FLYING CHANGES

Also by Maggie Dana

Keeping Secrets, Timber Ridge Riders (Book 1)
Racing into Trouble, Timber Ridge Riders (Book 2)
Riding for the Stars, Timber Ridge Riders (Book 3)
Wish Upon a Horse, Timber Ridge Riders (Book 4)
Chasing Dreams, Timber Ridge Riders (Book 5)
Almost Perfect, Timber Ridge Riders (Book 6)
Taking Chances, Timber Ridge Riders (Book 7)
After the Storm, Timber Ridge Riders (Book 8)
Double Feature, Timber Ridge Riders (Book 9)

Turning on a Dime ~ a time travel adventure
The Golden Horse of Willow Farm, Weekly Reader Books
Remember the Moonlight, Weekly Reader Books
Best Friends series, Troll Books

Sign up for our mailing list and be among the first to know when
the next Timber Ridge Riders book will be out.
Send your email address to:
timberridgeriders@gmail.com

For more information about the series, visit:
www.timberridgeriders.com
Note: all email addresses are kept strictly confidential.

TIMBER RIDGE RIDERS
∽ Book Ten ∾

FLYING CHANGES

Maggie Dana

PAGEWORKS PRESS

ISBN 978-0-9909498-0-0

Edited by Judith Cardanha
Cover by Margaret Sunter
Interior design by Anne Honeywood
Published by Pageworks Press
Text set in Sabon

for Noah and Sophie

1

A TANGLE OF JEANS, MISMATCHED SOCKS, and sparkly t-shirts lay sprawled across Holly Chapman's bed. On the other, her suitcase yawned open, overflowing with hoodies, breeches, underwear, and the two stuffed ponies Holly couldn't sleep without. Jennifer had told her and Kate to travel in their heaviest clothes.

"Why?" Holly had asked.

"So your luggage won't exceed the airline's weight limit."

Okaaaay . . . so did this mean flying to London in riding boots, leather chaps, and a helmet? With an exasperated sigh, Holly whipped the elastic off her blond pony tail and redid it. She'd never get through airport security dressed like a barn junkie. They'd think she was a total nut job, especially if she carried the umbrella that Jennifer also insisted on.

"It rains . . . a lot," Jennifer had warned.

"Should I bring foul-weather gear?" Holly asked. "Hip waders, a life vest?"

"Just an umbrella."

The only one Holly owned was lime green with froggy eyes. It matched the rubber boots she'd worn in first grade. Holly popped the umbrella open and almost jabbed herself in the eye with a broken rib.

"Yikes," said her best friend.

Holly whirled around as Kate stumbled through the door and promptly tripped over Holly's knapsack. Pencils, make-up, her iPod, and a fan magazine spilled out. Tubes of shampoo and conditioner rolled beneath her bed.

"Klutz," Holly said, grinning.

Kate's brown hair fell across one eye as she dropped to her knees and gathered up the mess. The magazine had a photo of Nathan Crane on its front cover, along with a splashy headline about the upcoming *Moonlight* premiere in London. Kate frowned, then looked at Holly, her green eyes wide with curiosity.

"Why are you bringing this?"

"To read on the plane," Holly said. "I'll be too nervous to sleep."

"Then why not bring those?" Kate said, waving toward an unwieldy pile of horse magazines on Holly's dresser.

"Yeah, okay," Holly said. "Good idea."

She grabbed a copy of *Young Rider*. It didn't matter which one as long as it distracted Kate. She was still on the floor, staring at her old boyfriend's familiar face, and Holly wondered for the millionth time if she was doing the right thing by not telling Kate about Nathan's invitation. He'd asked Adam, Holly's boyfriend, to fly over for the London premiere and was paying for his ticket. Adam wanted Holly to go with him, but she'd refused.

"You'll already be in England," Adam had argued. "So why not?"

"Because of Kate," Holly said. "And besides, we'll be in Cornwall, which is a bazillion miles from London."

"Idiot," Adam said. "It's a few hours by train."

But Holly refused to budge.

No way would she upset Kate by attending a fancy event that Kate hadn't been invited to. Not that Kate would care. Two months ago, she'd shocked the media and Nathan's fans by dumping him at the *Moonlight* premiere in New York and hadn't mentioned him since.

Until now.

Holly swapped out the magazines and stuffed Nathan Crane beneath a pillow. She'd read about him later, after Kate had gone home. "What did you pack?"

"Not much." Kate shrugged. "Jeans, t-shirts, my riding gear."

"That's all?"

"Yes," Kate said, looking puzzled. "What else do I need?"

"A dress? Pretty shoes?" Holly said.

Kate was totally hopeless with clothes. Her idea of getting dressed up meant clean breeches, a comfortable helmet, and socks that matched. At horse shows, she grumbled about having to wear a ratcatcher and always complained that the collars made her neck itch.

"A *dress*?" Kate said. "Why?"

"Duh-uh." Holly tossed her umbrella onto the bed. "Because this is England, stupid. They get dressed up over there, like for dinner and stuff. They don't slop about in shorts and bare feet."

"Even at the beach?"

Holly faked a shiver. "Only if it's warm enough."

Right now it was eighty degrees in Vermont, but Jennifer said that summer in England could be anything from bitterly cold to blisteringly hot, and that there was no air conditioning. So they should be prepared for anything.

"I don't *have* a dress," Kate said. "How about a jeans skirt? Won't that do?"

"No," Holly said.

Jennifer had been very specific. "Gran dresses for dinner every night," she'd said, even though her grandmother wore breeches and riding boots all day. "She'll expect us to do the same."

Caroline West, Jennifer's grandmother, had once been an Olympic rider and now owned Beaumont Park, one of England's finest equestrian centers. She'd invited Holly and Kate to join Jennifer at a special program for talented young riders. Jennifer, who lived at Timber Ridge for the school year, had already flown ahead to England. She would meet them at the airport in London.

The day after tomorrow.

Holly gulped. She'd never flown before. Kate had, but only on short hops with her father, except for a trip to England with her mom when Kate was almost nine. She said she barely remembered it. Holly double-checked to make sure she'd packed her brand-new passport where Kate wouldn't see it, along with her airline ticket, Jennifer's instructions about where to meet, and—

So much to remember.

"Let's go for a ride," Kate said.

* * *

Horses whickered and looked hopefully over stall doors as Kate and Holly entered the barn. Kate patted Daisy's black-and-white face, gave good old Marmalade a hug, and planted a kiss on Plug's cute little nose. He was the barn's smallest pony but made up for it by having the barn's biggest personality.

At Kate's birthday party in March, he'd gotten his rider eliminated from the apple-bobbing race by reaching the bucket first and scarfing up the apple himself. Kate slipped him a carrot, then headed for Tapestry's stall. Evening feed was long over, but it was still light enough to ride the trails that circled the base of Timber Ridge Mountain.

Quickly, they groomed and tacked up.

Kate wrapped her arms around Tapestry's neck. They'd never been parted for more than two days, but now they wouldn't see one another for a whole month.

"I wish you could come to England with me," Kate whispered into Tapestry's flaxen mane.

The chestnut mare nuzzled Kate's hand.

Kate fed her a carrot, then added an apple she'd only half eaten. Tapestry slobbered apple chunks and carrot juice down the front of Kate's t-shirt. In the next stall, Magician was frisking Holly's pockets while she put on his saddle.

When Jennifer first invited them to England, Kate and Holly had wanted to bring their horses.

"It's jolly expensive," Jennifer had said. "Like ten thousand dollars."

"Each way?" Kate said.

"Yup," Jennifer said. "But don't worry. My grandmother has fabulous horses, and you'll love them all."

Kate glanced across the aisle. Jennifer's chestnut gelding, Rebel, had his nose over his stall door, probably hoping for a treat. He'd gained quite a reputation with the younger kids for scarfing up vanilla pudding. His full brother, Renegade, who lived at Beaumont Park, preferred yogurt.

After tightening Tapestry's girth, Kate led her into the aisle and mounted. She joined Holly and Magician outside. They rode past the arena with its colorful jumps and headed for the trails. With luck they had another hour of daylight.

Holly gathered up her reins. "Let's do the hunt course."

"Okay, sure," Kate said.

It wasn't as tough as the cross-country course where she'd gotten in trouble last summer with Buccaneer. Against Liz's orders, Kate had raced him over the palisade, the railroad ties, and a water hazard because Angela Dean had taunted her with a challenge that Kate couldn't turn down. Buccaneer had performed brilliantly. But when Angela veered off course and jumped a stone wall topped with barbed wire, Kate had refused to follow.

Not on Buccaneer. Not on *any* horse.

You just didn't jump barbed wire, no matter how much you wanted to win and prove to Angela that Buccaneer wasn't the crazy horse that everyone else, including Holly, thought he was.

Kate still missed him.

Buccaneer loved peppermint Life Savers and had belonged to Giles Ballantine, the movie director, but he'd been sold on and nobody knew where he went. He was coal black, a mirror image of Magician, except Holly's horse was far more manageable than Buccaneer.

"He's a doppelgänger," Holly had declared shortly after Buccaneer arrived at Timber Ridge last summer. He'd exploded off the trailer snorting like a dragon. Even Liz had a hard time controlling him.

"Is that a warmblood?" Kate said. She'd never heard of a Doppelgänger before, but that didn't mean anything. Some of these German sport horses had really odd names like Oldenburg, Westphalian, and Trakehner.

Holly had laughed. "No, it's a shadow-self, like in *The Vampire Diaries*."

Kate had never watched it, but later she'd looked up *doppelgänger* on Wikipedia. Yes, that was Buccaneer, all right—Magician's almost twin.

* * *

A spectacular sunset painted the sky with mauve, pink and orange as both girls took turns on the Timber Ridge hunt course. Kate gave Tapestry her head, and they flew over brush jumps, rustic rails, and log piles as if they were no bigger than shoe boxes.

Slowing to a trot, Kate patted her mare's golden neck. She couldn't imagine loving a horse more than she loved Tapestry. Not even Magician came close, and Kate adored Holly's black gelding. He'd carried her to glory at the Hampshire Classic last summer. Together they'd helped to clinch victory for the riding team, and its gleaming trophy now took pride of place at the Timber Ridge club house.

But not for much longer.

In order to keep the challenge cup, a team had to win it three years in a row. So far, no team had—not even Larchwood, Timber Ridge's fiercest rival. Holly's boyfriend, Adam, rode for Larchwood but Holly was always nagging him to switch teams and ride for Timber Ridge instead.

As if reading Kate's mind, Holly said, "We're gonna miss the Hampshire Classic this year."

"I know," Kate said, feeling bad for Holly's mom who ran the barn and its riding team. With Kate, Holly, and Jennifer in England, Liz only had four riders to choose from. It would be a minor miracle if they won the trophy again.

"Think Angela will make it?" Holly said.

Tapestry shook her head to dislodge a deerfly, and Kate laughed. "There's your answer."

"No, seriously," Holly said. "She's hardly ridden Ragtime since—"

"The Festival of Horses?" Kate said.

It was the last show they'd attended, at the end of spring vacation. Angela had flubbed up so badly in front of her demanding mother and the U.S. Equestrian Federation talent scouts that she'd left the ring in tears and taken off. Nobody saw her again until Kate and Holly were being awarded a tie for fifth place.

Gleefully, they'd shared the pink ribbon.

Like they shared almost everything else—clothes, secrets, and even horses. Kate had ridden Magician at the Festival; Holly had ridden Tapestry. And now they were about to share a trip to Beaumont Park in England.

Kate couldn't wait to get there.

A whole month without Angela Dean and her bad attitude was the delicious frosting on top of an even more delicious cake—especially since Angela hadn't been invited to taste it.

2

BRAD PIRETTI'S GREEN EYES LIT UP when Kate and Holly returned to the barn. He ran a hand through his sandy brown
hair, then held Tapestry's reins while Kate dismounted,
almost as if he didn't trust her to manage without help.

"Good ride?" he said.

"Yeah," Kate replied. "We jumped the hunt course three
times."

Brad whistled. He'd been riding for less than six months
and hadn't progressed much beyond trotting over the cavalettis on Marmalade, the barn's biggest horse. Holly insisted
that Brad had taken up riding so he could hang out with
Kate.

"No way," Kate had argued. "He's just a friend."

Holly had rolled her eyes.

But right now, Brad's undivided attention made Kate feel
warm inside. He was sixteen—a year older than Kate—and

the high school's best quarterback. The cheerleaders adored him. So did the local snowboarding fans, who whooped and hollered whenever Brad swooshed down the Timber Ridge half-pipe, dazzling everyone with cannonballs, inverted rotations, and heart-stopping somersaults like an Olympic star.

This was something he shared with Kate. They both had big dreams—his for snowboarding, hers for three-day eventing. But Kate figured Brad had a better chance of success. He was already Vermont state champion in the half-pipe. Next winter he'd be going national. All he needed was a fancier snowboard.

If Kate wanted to realize her dream, she'd have to sell Tapestry and trade up to a more expensive horse with better training, which was what many riders did if they were serious about making it to the top. For them, horses were dispensable, like snowboards. But not for Kate.

A tear trickled down her cheek.

"I'll miss you," she mumbled into Tapestry's mane. More tears erupted. She wiped them away, but not before Brad noticed.

"I'll miss you, too," he whispered.

Turning away to hide her blush, Kate blushed even harder when Brad leaned against Tapestry and sandwiched her gently between himself and her horse. She couldn't move.

Not that she wanted to.

There was a refreshing honesty about Brad Piretti that Nathan Crane lacked. Last year when Kate first met Nathan, everyone had fawned over him, even Holly's Aunt Bea, who spotted phonies faster than hounds scented a fox. But all that changed in New York when Kate discovered that Nathan Crane was nothing more than a figment of his own imagination and the studio's publicity department.

"When are you coming back?" Brad asked.

"Middle of July."

"So, four weeks."

"Pretty much," Kate replied.

She and Holly were missing the last three days of school so they could be in England with plenty of time to get settled before the intensive riding program began. Jennifer said there would be eight students, all crackerjack riders and chosen carefully by her grandmother.

"Crackerjack?" Holly had said. "Us?"

"You bet," Jennifer said. "And my gran is never wrong."

* * *

Brad drove Kate home. It seemed to take longer than usual, and when Kate glanced at the dashboard, she saw that he was driving well below the speed limit.

"Is something wrong with the truck?" she said. It was pretty beat up with a dented fender, wonky headlights, and rusty bumpers, but it normally went faster than this.

He shot her a crooked grin. "You rumbled me."

"I *what*?"

"I'm driving slowly, on purpose," Brad said, maneuvering carefully past an old red tractor with narrow wheels that looked as if it belonged in a museum. The farmer waved.

Kate waved back. "Why?"

"Because I won't see you for a month, and—"

Kate caught her breath. She knew Brad liked her. He'd made that pretty obvious, but she didn't know how to handle it. Holly told her to relax and go with the flow, but having made such a mess of her relationship with Nathan, Kate was nervous about jumping into another one. Plus it seemed kind of pointless to get involved with a guy and leave him for a month while she flew off to England.

Brakes squealed as Brad pulled up in front of Kate's cottage. Her father had rented it from his sister, but when Aunt Marion returned from North Carolina in July, they'd have to move. Kate had no idea where they'd be living next. So far, her father hadn't had any luck finding them another house—not in Winfield, anyway.

For a moment, Kate stared out the window. She twisted her hands together, then sat on them and counted the squashed bugs on Brad's windshield. Then she counted the rose bushes in Aunt Marion's front garden. The bugs won.

Brad said, "Guess I'd better clean it, huh?"

He sounded as awkward as she felt. Was he going to kiss her? He'd kissed her twice before—once on the ski slope and then again after she won her ribbon at the Festival of Horses.

It seemed okay then.

But it didn't seem quite so okay now.

"I'd better go," Kate said. "Dad will be waiting."

Except he wasn't. He was working late at his butterfly museum so he could take tomorrow off and drive them to the airport in Boston. Liz was coming, too.

Brad leaned over.

Slipping his arm around Kate's shoulders he drew her closer. She stiffened, then relaxed. This was Brad, a guy she trusted. He mucked stalls, cleaned tack, and cheered the riding team at horse shows. His lips landed on hers.

Wow.

It was just as good as the last time he'd done it. Even better.

Kate was trying to pluck up enough courage to kiss him back, when two of Brad's football buddies sauntered past. One of them whistled and banged on the truck's hood; the other gave Brad a thumbs-up. Reluctantly, Kate pulled herself free. This would be all over school tomorrow, and thank goodness she wouldn't be there to deal with it.

"Morons," Brad said. "They're jealous."

The guys walked off laughing and shoving one another. Kate felt another blush creep up her face. If anyone ever invented a blush blocker, she'd be first in line to buy it. Scooping her knapsack off the floor, she reached for the door handle.

"Wait up," Brad said.

Kate turned. "Why?"

"This." Brad shifted closer, pressed his cheek against hers, and held his iPhone at arm's length. "Smile."

"Too late," Kate said, blinking.

Brad shot another. "Better?"

At least her eyes were open, but she still looked kind of goofy, like a deer caught in headlights. "I guess."

"What's your address?"

Without thinking, Kate said, "Number ten, Elm—"

"Your e-mail, silly."

Up came another blush as Kate recited her e-mail address and watched Brad's enormous thumbs fly over the keypad without making a single mistake. Seconds later, her phone gave a muffled ping from the depths of her knapsack.

"Mission accomplished," Brad said, grinning. "Do you want me to brush Tapestry while you're gone? Take her for a walk, or something?"

"Yes, and thank you," Kate said. "But check with Liz because she's going to let Marcia ride her."

Brad raised an eyebrow. "Angela's kid sister?"

"Ex-stepsister," Kate corrected.

The Deans had gotten a divorce and Marcia now lived in New York with her dad. But she would be up for the summer to stay with her best friend Laura Gardner. Both girls were eleven and they worshipped Tapestry, especially when Kate made her lie down on command.

The barn's younger kids loved this trick.

It had helped save Marcia's life when she got lost in the Halloween blizzard. Holly and Kate had found her, and while Holly rode off to get help, Kate and Tapestry had snuggled with Marcia to keep her from freezing.

"I should go," Kate said, not wanting to.

"Text me?" Brad said. "Send pictures?"

Kate swallowed hard. "Okay."

She ran up the front steps. Persy, Aunt Marion's black

cat, curled himself around her legs, meowing as if he hadn't been fed for a week. Kate turned. Brad gave her a jaunty wave with his phone and pulled away. Feeling awkward, she waved back. Why had she run off? Why hadn't she sat in the truck and talked to him? Holly would've been yammering until midnight.

There was a note from Dad on the kitchen table.

Back around ten. Dinner's in the fridge.

Suddenly starving, Kate yanked it open to find one of her favorites, pasta salad with avocados and cherry tomatoes. Dad wasn't exactly a domestic god, but he'd turned into a pretty good cook thanks to the lessons Kate and Holly had bought him and Liz for Christmas in the hopes of getting them together, like in Holly's favorite movie *The Parent Trap*.

So far, it seemed to be working.

Dad was teaching Liz about butterflies, she was doing her best to get him interested in horses, and they'd both ganged up on the girls about curfews and homework—just like regular parents did.

Holly dreamed of a fairytale wedding.

She had visions of her and Kate as bridesmaids in clouds of pink chiffon with daisies and ribbons in their hair. Liz and Ben would exchange vows beneath a bower of pink roses, then leave for their honeymoon in a gold carriage pulled by a pair of gleaming white horses.

"We don't have any white horses," Kate had pointed out.

They didn't even have any horses trained to pull a carriage, except for Marmalade, and he barely moved. If you wanted him to trot on Thursday, you had to mention it on Monday so he'd have time to think about it.

"No problem," Holly replied. "We'll use pink unicorns instead."

* * *

The airport hummed with activity. Loudspeakers blared, screens blinked, and lines of weary passengers with over-stuffed suitcases shuffled toward a bank of check-in desks. In the concourse, people parted like a wave as airline crews in smart uniforms strode along, pulling identical black bags and looking terribly official.

Kate had seen all this before, but Holly hadn't. As they rode up the escalator, she shot anxious glances through floor-to-ceiling windows at the enormous airplanes hitched up to jetways and waiting to be filled with passengers, including her.

Then came security—another endless line.

"We can't come any further," Mom said, and scooped Holly into a hug. She handed her a small silver box and gave another, exactly the same, to Kate. "Promise to call the minute you guys arrive."

"Okay," Holly said. "But what's this?"

Kate was already opening hers. "A bracelet?"

"From Tapestry's mane," Mom said, grinning. "Aunt Bea made it."

"Mine, too?" Holly pulled a braided black circle from its nest of white tissue and slipped it onto her wrist. A perfect fit.

"Just a reminder," Mom said. "Of Magician."

As if Holly needed one. She threw her arms around Mom, and then Kate joined the hug fest, followed by her dad. His beard tickled Holly's cheek.

For a moment, her eyes filled with tears.

Her own father had died three years before in a car accident that left Holly temporarily paralyzed. Dad was irreplaceable, but Kate's father would come really close to filling his shoes—if Mom came to her senses and married him.

Liz and Ben had become good friends—like going on dates and stuff—and as they all hugged for one last time, Holly allowed herself to think it might actually happen. Then she and Kate would be sisters—real sisters—instead of pretending they were.

But, as Kate kept reminding her, blended families didn't always work the way you wanted them to. Just look at Marcia and Angela—*Cinderella and her spiteful stepsister.*

Holly gave a little shudder.

No, it wouldn't happen to them. Their parents would get married, and they'd all live happily ever after, never mind if she and Kate argued about boys and movies or squabbled over whose turn it was to use the shower first.

3

THE AIRPLANE BOUNCED THROUGH a patch of turbulence, and Kate's eyes flew open. For a moment, she didn't know where she was. The cabin lights had been dimmed, and beside her, Holly was sprawled across two seats, snuggled up with pillows and a soft blanket.

Holly yawned. "What time is it?"

"Four-thirty," Kate said.

"Morning or afternoon?"

"Morning, silly." Kate glanced at the seat-belt sign and fastened hers, then adjusted her watch because London was five hours ahead of Vermont.

Rubbing her eyes, Holly sat up. "Let's watch a movie."

"Okay, which one?"

Kate had looked through the airline's selection but hadn't found anything that got her heart started—well, except for *Moonlight*, and she'd already seen it. In fact, she'd actually

19

been *in* it, riding as a stunt double for Nathan's co-star, Tess O'Donnell, when part of the film was shot at Timber Ridge last summer. But Holly wanted to watch it again. So they put on their earphones and fired up the screens on the backs of the seats in front of them.

Kate's attention wandered.

She read snippets of *Dressage Today* and played *Angry Birds* on her iPhone. But when Holly nudged her, she looked up.

"It's *you*," Holly whispered.

Dressed as Ophelia Brown in a flowing white gown and pursued by zombies, Kate galloped Magician toward the camera. Behind her came Ian Hamilton—the movie's dashing hero—riding a flashy pinto. As he gathered Ophelia into his arms, the screen faded to black.

Holly sighed. "He's *so* cute."

"Duh-uh," Kate said. "It's Adam, remember?"

He was Nathan's stunt double as well as his best friend. With the same green eyes and floppy hair, they looked so much alike that they'd often swapped clothes in junior high school and confused their teachers.

"Another doppelgänger," Holly said.

Now that she knew what it meant, Kate nodded. If you looked at separate photos of Nathan and Adam, it was hard to tell them apart. But if you really knew them, the differences were obvious. Adam was funny, sweet, and honest. Nathan was . . . well, he'd changed a lot since last summer, and Kate didn't want to travel down that road again.

A cabin attendant stopped by with coffee, warm pastries, and orange juice. She glanced at Holly's screen.

"I *love* that movie."

"Me, too," Holly said. "And my friend is in it."

"Really?" the attendant said, almost spilling coffee on Kate's lap.

"She's a famous movie star," Holly said, with a perfectly straight face. "But don't tell anyone, okay? We're traveling incognito."

Kate wanted to strangle her.

She'd pulled this crazy trick on the saleslady at Blaines, an exclusive boutique in the village where they'd bought their dresses for *Moonlight*'s New York premiere. The studio had paid for them, and now Kate's iridescent blue gown with its scratchy shawl was stuffed into her suitcase in the hopes it would do for dinner at Beaumont Park.

She'd also shoved in a jeans skirt and an old t-shirt dress she had found at the back of her closet—just to be on the safe side, because Holly didn't always get it right. Neither did Jennifer whose spiky hair was a different color every week, to say nothing of her odd assortment of clothes. One day she'd showed up at the barn wearing green cargo pants, a sparkly purple tank top, and long striped socks that made her look like a punk version of Raggedy Ann.

As the airplane made its gradual descent toward Heathrow Airport, Kate peered through the window, amazed at how lush and green everything was. Black-and-white cows grazed in a patchwork of fields; cottonball sheep dotted the rolling hills. From up here it looked like the toy farm she'd played with as a child. A sudden movement caught her eye.

"Look," she said to Holly.

Below them, two foals frisked about under the watchful eyes of their mothers.

Wow.

Kate loved England already.

* * *

After what seemed like ten miles of corridors, escalators, and people movers, Kate and Holly finally arrived at Customs and Immigration. Trying not to yawn, they stood in yet another endless line.

"Enjoy your stay in England," said a cheerful official as he stamped their passports. Holly snatched hers back as soon as he was done with it.

"Let me see it," Kate said.

Holly had moaned and groaned about having to get a passport and fill out all the paperwork, but she'd never shown it to Kate, like it was some kind of big secret.

Holly stuffed the passport into her bag. "Later."

"What are you here for?" the man said.

"Olympic dreams," Holly said.

The man frowned. "That was two years ago."

"Then I guess we're a bit late."

"Hush," Kate warned. It wasn't a good idea to be flip with officials, especially at airports when armed guards were hanging about. Kate whipped out her phone to call Dad. No service.

That was odd.

Around her, others were talking on ear pieces and cell phones. Maybe hers didn't work because of some weird setting that needed to be turned on. With a shrug, Kate shoved it back inside her pocket and followed the signs for baggage claim. More crowds to deal with. Apologizing profusely, Kate maneuvered her way to the front and snatched their suitcases from the carousel.

"Now what?" Holly said.

"We find Jennifer."

Except she wasn't there. Kate scanned the crowd at Arrivals, but all she could see was a tall, gray-haired woman in a trench coat and Wellington boots with a cardboard sign that said *Timber Ridge Riders*.

"That's us," Holly said, jumping up and down.

The woman waved and strode toward them. She held out her hand. "Welcome to England. I'm Judith West."

Aunt Judith?

Kate shot a look at Holly. They'd both heard Jennifer's stories about her grandmother's amazing sister who'd abandoned her British upbringing at eighteen and run off to America, where she joined a rodeo. For nine months Aunt Judith had toured the country riding broncs, performing back bends and flips on horseback, and jumping mustangs through flaming circles.

"Did you meet Buffalo Bill?" Holly said. "Calamity Jane?"

Aunt Judith smiled. "They were a bit before my time. Now, come along. We've got a lot to do."

"Where's Jennifer?" Kate said, struggling to keep up with Aunt Judith whose legs appeared to be twice as long as hers.

"Working in the yard," Aunt Judith said. "We're short-handed, so Caroline asked me to meet you instead."

"Yard?" Holly said. "Like in vegetables?"

Kate had visions of Jennifer pulling weeds and planting tomatoes, or maybe pruning roses like the ones in Aunt Marion's garden.

Aunt Judith laughed. "Over here, a yard is a stable."

"Not a garden?" Kate said.

"No." Aunt Judith stopped and turned so abruptly that Kate almost ran into her. "We've got a whole day to kill, so are you girls ready for a little sightseeing?"

"Yes," Kate said, "but first I need to call home."

Except the call still wouldn't go through. Kate tried her phone and then Holly's and got nothing but silence.

Aunt Judith offered hers. "Here you go."

"Thanks." But that didn't work, either.

"There are phone shops everywhere," said Aunt Judith. "We'll find one later."

* * *

After breakfast at an airport café, they took the subway into London, except Aunt Judith called it the *tube*. At every stop, a disembodied voice warned passengers to "Mind the gap."

"Where are we going?" Holly couldn't stop yawning and desperately needed a nap, but she didn't want to miss a single minute. She popped a peppermint candy into her mouth. Maybe that would help wake her up.

"Paddington."

"Like the bear?" Kate said.

"The one and only," said Aunt Judith. "We'll leave your luggage at the station, and then we'll explore. Tonight we take the sleeper train to Cornwall. But first we have to find the princess."

"*Princess*?" Holly squealed.

This was getting cooler and cooler by the minute. First her favorite bear and *now* a princess? But there was no time to stop and admire the statue of Paddington. Aunt Judith waved vaguely toward it, then arranged with a concierge for the girls' luggage to be delivered to the sleeper train that night. As soon as they reached the street, she put two fingers in her mouth and let out a shrill whistle.

"Yikes," Holly said, covering her ears.

A large black taxi pulled up. "Where to, Ma'am?"

"The Royal Mews," said Aunt Judith, as if it were the most normal thing in the world. She ushered the girls inside and sat opposite them on a fold-down jump seat.

"Muse?" Holly said. "Like you're supposed to get when you write an essay?"

"No, *m-e-w-s*," said Aunt Judith, laughing. "It's where the queen keeps her carriage horses and the state coaches. We're meeting the princess there."

Holly glanced at Aunt Judith's muddy boots and her raincoat with its torn pockets, missing buttons, and empty belt loops. Not exactly the best outfit for meeting royalty.

Then again, she and Kate didn't look too sharp either. Kate's wrinkled shirt had come untucked and part of Holly's breakfast had landed in her lap. Good thing she wasn't wearing her brand new chaps, or they'd have been ruined.

* * *

A warden looking crisply smart in a navy-and-red uniform guided them and several others around the Royal Mews at Buckingham Palace. Glittering chandeliers hung from the domed ceiling; fluted white columns flanked the spotless aisle. On both sides were well-groomed carriage horses. They wore matching halters, and even their forelocks seemed to fall at just the same spot on their handsome grey faces. There wasn't a speck of dirt to be seen. If a horse pooped, a groom was there within seconds to clean it up.

Kate wanted to help.

Her hands itched to grab a pitchfork or a broom—even a muck bucket. It wasn't right to be in a stable full of horses and not doing anything.

"I know how you feel," said Aunt Judith.

Smoothly, their guide steered them toward the state coaches—a stunning display of gold wheels, gleaming bodywork, and crystal lamps etched with the royal coat of arms. The Diamond Jubilee State Coach was eighteen feet long, weighed almost three tons, and had electronic windows.

"Does it have Wi-Fi?" Holly asked.

As if on cue, Aunt Judith's phone chirped. She reached into her canvas bag and pulled it out, then punched several buttons. "I'm no good with this infernal contraption," she said, handing it to Holly. "Can you figure it out?"

"Sure." Holly peered at the tiny screen. "You've got a text."

"A message?" said Aunt Judith.

"Yes," said Holly.

This was something else Jennifer had told them about Aunt Judith. She was brilliant with horses but hopeless with technology and stubbornly refused to learn it. "She still writes letters by hand," Jennifer had said. "And then she gets on her bike and takes them to the village post office."

"What does it say?" said Aunt Judith.

Holly glanced down. "Meet us at London Eye—Steffan."

"Who's that?" Kate said. "And what's an *eye*?"

"It's a gigantic Ferris wheel," Aunt Judith said. "And Steffan is Princess Isabel's bodyguard."

* * *

Over fish and chips in Covent Garden, Aunt Judith told them about Isabel DuBois, whose father was tenth in line for the throne of Lunaberg.

"Is that a real country?" Kate said.

"It used to be," said Aunt Judith, "a long time ago. But it got swallowed up when Europe reshuffled itself after the Napoleonic wars."

Kate had read about this in school. Some countries had real kings and queens, like England, Sweden, and the Netherlands. Others had tossed off the old regimes and turned into republics, like the United States, but a few still had pretenders to their long-vanished thrones.

"Like Bonnie Prince Charlie?" she said.

"Yes," Aunt Judith said. "But don't say that in front of Mr. MacDonald. He's a Scot, and it's a sore point with him." She pushed her plate to one side. "Mac's been our stable manager for years and we all think he walks on water. So don't upset him—even if you can't understand his accent."

"What about Isabel?" Kate said. "Does she speak English?"

"Better than you." Aunt Judith grinned. "She was born in London with a silver spoon in her mouth."

"Literally?" Holly said.

"No, it means that her family is really well off. They're also a bit toffee-nosed, and—"

"Toffee-nosed?" Kate said.

"Stuck up," Aunt Judith said. "Think they're better than anyone else."

"But can Isabel ride?" Kate said and felt instantly stupid. Of course, the girl could ride. Jennifer said they were all crackerjacks, didn't she?

Even so, Aunt Judith hesitated. She picked up her coffee, and then put it down again as if she needed time to think of the right words. "Isabel's had the best ponies and the best instructors."

It wasn't an answer, and Kate didn't have a chance to pursue it because the waiter arrived with their check and Aunt Judith announced they were going to Horse Guards Parade, but first they'd be visiting the British Museum.

Holly groaned. "Aunt Judith, we—"

"Before you go any further, let's get one thing clear," said Aunt Judith holding up her hand. "Don't call me *Aunt Judith*. I'm Jude to everyone, including you. Got it?"

"What was your show name?" Kate said. Somehow, *Judith West* seemed too staid for the rodeo circuit.

For a moment, Jude's smile turned wistful, and Kate had a glimpse of the younger woman she'd once been, riding fearlessly on half-broke horses, roping steers, and jumping through rings of fire.

"It was the late nineteen sixties," she said. "So, take a guess."

"*Hey Jude?*" Holly said.

"Right on," said Jennifer's great aunt, giving Holly a fist bump. "You actually *like* The Beatles?"

"Who doesn't?"

"Most kids your age don't even know who they are," said Jude. "They're all into hip-hop and boy bands."

"Not Holly," Kate said. "She's a walking encyclopedia about old music—and old movies."

They left the café with Holly singing *Hey Jude* from beginning to end. Aunt Judith—no, *Jude*—praised Holly for getting all the words right.

4

To Kate's relief, they bypassed the museum and took a taxi to Horse Guards Parade. As they drove along Piccadilly, it seemed to Kate as if Nathan Crane's face was everywhere—on billboards, in shop windows, and even on the red double-decker buses with banner ads for the *Moonlight* premiere on their sides.

Except it wasn't a real premiere—not like the one in New York—because the film was already in movie theaters. Holly had figured this out after reading her latest fan magazine. It was, she said, an excuse for the director, Giles Ballantine, to throw himself another extravagant party. Kate shivered.

Thank goodness she wasn't going.

Apart from a few tourists, Horse Guards Parade was deserted—no horses and no guards—just a lone soldier in a sentry box looking stiff and stern beneath his plumed helmet. Its heavy gold chinstrap covered most of his mouth.

"They're not allowed to smile," said Jude.

"Ever?" Holly said.

"Not on duty."

A little boy ran up to the guard, touched his sword, and ran back to his parents. The guard didn't move, but Holly insisted she saw his lips twitch. A middle-aged couple, looking faintly ridiculous in Bermuda shorts, flip-flops, and flowery shirts, had their photo taken standing on either side of the guard.

Holly gave Jude her iPhone. "Do you know how to take a picture?"

"Barely."

"Just point and click," Holly said, then grabbed Kate's hand. "C'mon."

Reluctantly, Kate went with her. She felt sorry for the guard, who had to be roasting inside his scarlet jacket and black boots that came halfway up his thighs. How on earth did he ride in those things, never mind walk? They were taller than dressage boots.

Holly told him they'd just arrived from the States that very morning and that they rode in three-day events, and she wanted to know if he'd ever done that with his horse. The guard didn't move a muscle—just kept staring straight ahead at Jude, who somehow managed to take a photo.

"It's perfect," Holly said. But when she tried to send it to Adam, nothing happened. "I guess we need the phone store."

They found one at Westminster Bridge, near the Houses

of Parliament and Big Ben, London's most famous landmark. Obligingly, it chimed.

Three o'clock.

Kate yawned. With no sleep on the plane, she'd been awake for more than twenty-four hours and doubted she'd sleep on the train to Cornwall, either. Across the river was the biggest Ferris wheel she'd ever seen.

"Is that the London Eye?"

"Some call it the London *Eyesore*," Jude said with a grin, "and we'll ride it later, then meet up with Isabel. But first we need to solve your phone trauma." She ushered them into the store where a sales assistant told Holly she needed a different SIM card.

Kate handed over her phone as well, followed by the credit card her father had given her. This was the first time she'd ever used it, and she felt guilty and grown-up, all at the same time.

"Is ten pounds all right?" the guy said, pulling out their old cards.

"What for?"

"The new card," he said. "It's prepaid."

"Better make it twenty," Jude said. "It costs quite a bit to call the States."

They settled on fifteen pounds for Kate and twenty-five for Holly because she'd be texting with Adam a bazillion times a day. Kate wondered if she'd hear from Brad. She hoped so. But first, she had to call her father.

He answered on the first ring. "Where are you?"

"London," Kate said. "With Jennifer's aunt. We had to swap the SIM cards in our phones because—"

Dad interrupted. "Are you okay?"

"Yes, we're fine," Kate said, yawning. "Just tired."

"Liz is here," he said. "I'm at the barn and we've been—"

"Dad," Kate yelled. "Is Tapestry all right?"

"Of course, she is," Dad said. "It's you we're worried about. Now put Holly on."

After assuring her mother that no, they had not been abducted, and yes, they were having a wonderful time, Holly rang off with a promise to call later. She gave the phone back to Kate. "Let's go to Harrods."

"What's that?"

"Just about *the* most exclusive store in the whole wide world," Holly said, eyes shining so bright that Kate could almost see her reflection.

* * *

They rode the top of a double-decker bus to Knightsbridge, where Harrods took up an entire block. Parked at the curb, Kate counted a dozen super-expensive sports cars—Jaguars, Aston Martins, and BMWs—in all the colors of a box of crayons. There was even a hot pink Ferrari.

"Adam would love this," Holly said.

Bowing stiffly, a doorman in dark green livery and a top hat welcomed them to Harrods.

"Do you think he rides dressage?" Holly whispered.

Kate giggled. "Ask him."

So Holly did, but the man shook his head. "What's dressage, miss?"

Jude gave her a gentle push. "Not everyone in England is horse crazy. Come on, we've got a lot to see."

They cruised through Harrods's famous food halls with their tantalizing displays of delicacies from all over the world, then rode the shiny escalators to floors filled with designer clothes only royalty and movie stars could possibly afford. Holly fell in love with a skinny leather belt.

"I could *so* use this," she said, buckling it around her waist.

Kate read the price tag. "Two hundred pounds."

"How much is that in real money?"

"Three hundred and forty dollars," Kate said. She'd checked the conversion rate before they left Vermont. Right now, an English pound was worth one dollar and seventy-two cents.

Holly dropped the belt. "Ouch."

Jude brought them down to earth in a huge elevator lined with etched glass and hammered bronze panels, except she called it a *lift*. Kate's head was already buzzing with all the new words to remember—*yard* for stable, *tube* for subway, and *chips* for french fries.

Back in the food hall, Jude bought individual meat pies, three bottles of ginger beer, and a wedge of cheese. "For a picnic on the South Bank," she said. "Then we'll ride the Eye."

Kate yawned.

"That is, if you can stay awake long enough," Jude added.

* * *

From atop the enormous wheel, Holly looked down. Not a good idea. She'd never been up this high before, except in the airplane. Not even the chairlifts at Timber Ridge Mountain went this far off the ground. She felt a little dizzy. But the view was awesome—lit up like fairyland as far as she could see.

Jude pointed out the Tower of London, St. Paul's Cathedral, and a skyscraper shaped like a pickle that Londoners had nicknamed the "Gherkin." And, of course, Big Ben. It chimed ten o'clock.

"Time for us to go," Jude said. "Our train leaves at midnight."

"Go where?" Holly said.

The wheel had stopped. They weren't moving at all except to swing imperceptibly in the breeze, and their capsule was all the way at the top of the Eye's enormous arc. Kate didn't seem the least bit fazed. She stood by the window looking down and asking Jude if they could see Greenwich because that's where the Olympic equestrian events had been held.

Minutes ticked by.

Somewhere, down below, Holly heard a siren. Was that a police car? An ambulance? One of the other passengers said it was probably someone having a panic attack and being taken off the Eye.

Holly felt close to a panic attack herself.

Then, with a gentle lurch, the wheel set off again, slowly downward. Holly heaved a sigh of relief. She couldn't wait to get off, to have her feet firmly planted on the ground. Funny, but she never felt this way about being on a horse. Maybe it was because they had their feet—all four of them—on the ground. Well, most of the time.

"You okay?" Kate said, sounding anxious.

Holly swallowed hard. "Yeah."

It took another twenty minutes to reach the bottom. As they were getting out of their capsule, Jude's cell phone rang. She held it to her ear for a moment, then frowned and handed it to Holly.

"It's Isabel, but I think I cut her off."

"Woops," Holly said. "Want me to call her back?"

"Please."

But it was easier said than done. All of a sudden, Holly's fingers turned into lumps of clay and she couldn't find the right buttons. Her heart skipped a beat. In a couple of seconds she'd be talking to a real live princess.

Isabel.

Belle?

Just like *Beauty and the Beast*.

Maybe they'd become best friends and Holly would be invited for sleepovers in a castle with turrets and a moat. There'd be hunt balls and snazzy cars like the ones they saw outside Harrods and all the other cool stuff she'd read about in her magazines, like rock stars giving private concerts and—

The phone rang again. "Hello?"

"You cut me *off*," said an imperious voice.

Holly opened her mouth and shut it again. Then she dropped the phone into Jude's outstretched hand as if it had suddenly turned smoking hot.

* * *

The conversation lasted less than a minute. With a sigh bordering on exasperation, Jude pocketed her phone. "Isabel's bodyguard is in hospital," she said, waving at a taxi. "He's the one they took off the Eye."

"Panic attack?" Kate said.

She couldn't imagine a bodyguard being afraid of a Ferris wheel. Then again, some people, no matter how tough they were, hated heights—like Holly, who was the bravest person Kate knew. Last summer when Holly was still stuck in her wheelchair, she'd rescued Buccaneer from a barn fire, and then she'd confounded her doctors—and everyone else—by learning to walk and ride again.

"Yes," Jude said, as a blue minicab did an illegal U-turn and screeched to a halt in front of them. "But they're keeping him overnight for observation. Isabel's gone home. She'll come down to Cornwall tomorrow, so we needn't have wasted a whole day hanging about. It was her idea to ride the sleeper train, not mine."

"Where does she live?" Kate said.

"All over the place," Jude said, climbing into the cab. "London, Bermuda, Paris—"

"That's a bit beyond my range," said the driver.

Jude grinned. "Then we'll settle for Paddington, and make it fast. We've got a train to catch."

"Don't we all," he said.

"Where does the princess keep her horse?" Kate said as London flashed by at a dizzying speed. With Hyde Park on their left, they barreled up Park Lane, and Kate had visions of Isabel riding sidesaddle along Rotten Row, like the aristocrats did many years ago—women in frilly bonnets and long velvet gowns, men wearing top hats and tails.

"Right now he's with her trainer," Jude said. "He's got a yard close to Dartmoor."

"Oh, can we go?" Holly said. "I'd love to see the wild ponies." She scrunched up her nose. "Is Princess Isabel's horse a Dartmoor?"

"Dartmoors are ponies," Kate said. "Not three-day-event horses."

"I *know*," Holly said, sounding annoyed. "That was a joke."

At the next traffic light, their cab driver hung a left and zoomed into Paddington Station so fast that Kate was convinced they'd end up on the platform, maybe on the train itself. Jude paid the driver and delivered a stern lecture about reckless driving.

"Gemini's a Dutch Warmblood," she said, as their driver took off even faster than he'd arrived.

Holly said, "Just like Angela's horse."

"Who's Angela?"

Kate almost blurted, *Princess Isabel's doppelgänger*, but stopped herself in time. Somehow, it sounded kind of silly. "One of the girls we ride with at Timber Ridge."

5

A MOTHERLY LOOKING WOMAN whose name tag said "Margaret" ushered them on board a navy blue train with *Night Riviera Sleeper* written on its side.

"What about our luggage?" Holly said. "Our riding gear?"

"All taken care of," Jude replied.

And there it was, stacked neatly in an alcove, boots and helmets lined up on shelves above. Margaret led them down a narrow corridor with windows on the left and sleeper cabins on the right. She opened a door. "There you are, my love."

"Wow," Kate said. "This is so cool."

There were two bunk beds with crisp white sheets, a tiny sink, and barely enough room to turn around. But who cared? With luck, they'd be asleep in five seconds and wouldn't wake up till they got to Cornwall.

Margaret said, "I'll be serving you ladies breakfast about thirty minutes before you arrive. Now what would you like?" She handed out menus.

Holly opted for croissants, yogurt, and strawberry jam. "Lots of jam."

"Eggs and bacon for me," Kate said. "Please."

Jude said, "Just coffee, and strong."

"I'm glad Isabel's not here," Kate said as soon as they shut the door to their cabin. Jude was in the next one, but Kate didn't think she'd be able to hear them over the rumbling noises their train made as it left the station.

"So am I."

"Seriously?" Kate said.

Holly nodded, but Kate wasn't convinced. Her best friend loved glamour and glitz and anything that sparkled, and she was probably crushed that the princess wasn't joining them for the overnight journey. Maybe Holly would've wanted to share a cabin with Isabel instead of with Kate. On the other hand, if Isabel had come along, she'd have been in a royal carriage all by herself . . . well, except for her bodyguard.

Kate had visions of the bodyguard sleeping on a mattress outside the princess's door. She yawned, then giggled.

"What?" Holly said.

Kate shrugged. "Nothing. I'm tired."

"Me, too." Holly climbed into the top bunk and peered over the edge like Snoopy on his doghouse, the way she had when they shared a room at the Festival of Horses. "G'night."

Kate brushed her teeth and fell into bed. She was asleep five seconds after her head hit the pillow.

* * *

As promised, Margaret delivered breakfast along with the news that they'd be arriving at St. Austell in twenty-nine minutes. The weather was a bit cloudy but quite warm for this time of year. Kate ran into Jude on her way to the tiny toilet at the end of their carriage.

"Sleep okay?" Jude said.

Kate yawned. "Like a rock."

At six-thirty, they gathered up their luggage and stepped off the train. Kate's suitcase got stuck in the door. A wiry man with bowed legs pulled it free.

"Girls, this is Mr. MacDonald," Jude said.

He tipped his cap. "'Mac' will do just fine."

But when Kate introduced herself, his steely gray eyes narrowed. "McGregor, you say. Now would that be the highland McGregors or the lowland McGregors?" His accent was so thick, Kate could barely understand him.

"I have no clue," she said. "We're just the American McGregors."

"Emigrants," Mac muttered. "But that's all right, I suppose. Are ye sheep farmers?"

"No," Kate said. "My father's an entomologist."

"Bugs?"

"Butterflies," Kate said, and regretted it immediately. It made Dad sound like a little boy catching Monarchs with a

net on Sunday afternoons rather than a highly regarded professor who'd led scientific expeditions to the Amazon jungle.

Mac made a harrumphing noise and turned toward
Holly, but she got there first. "I'm Holly Chapman, and, no,
I wasn't named after a bush." She gave him a defiant stare,
then looked down. Almost inaudibly she said, "My middle
name is Hollister, but—"

Kate gasped. *Hollister?*

Why hadn't Holly told her? And what was her first name
if it wasn't *Holly?* Feeling somehow betrayed, Kate dragged
her suitcase toward the Beaumont Park van and clambered
into the rear seat. Holly got in the middle seat with Jude,
which was good because right now Kate didn't feel like sitting next to her.

* * *

After leaving the station, they drove south on country lanes
so narrow that when they met an oncoming vehicle one of
them had to back up into a gateway to let the other pass.
Now and then a break in the tall hedges afforded spectacular
views of rolling meadows, small villages, and an occasional
glimpse of silvery sand and shimmering blue water.

"How far is the beach?" Holly asked.

"Close enough," Mac said, as he pulled up behind a herd
of brown-and-white cows that blocked the road. The farmer
tipped his cap, then poked a straggler with his stick. Lazily,
the cow flicked its tail and shot the farmer a baleful look.

"Cornish traffic jam," Jude said.

It took another ten minutes for the farmer and his
Guernseys to reach their destination. As Mac patiently
inched the van forward, Kate glanced out the rear window.
Behind them was a stream of cars and trucks, but nobody
honked. If this had happened back home, drivers would be
making rude gestures and complaining.

Life was slower here, and Kate loved it.

She loved it even more when Mac pulled into the drive-
way that led to Beaumont Park. It was just as gorgeous as the
photos in its glossy brochure that Kate had looked at so
many times it was now a crumpled mess in her knapsack.

Through a rose-covered archway Kate saw an old stone
house with multiple chimneys and ivy growing up the walls.
Fanning out from both sides were brick stable blocks that
formed a U-shape with the house. Each stall had two doors—
one overlooking the yard and another that looked out back
onto lush green fields, two riding rings, and a huge indoor
arena.

Morning feed was in full swing.

Horses whinnied and banged on stall doors. Grooms in
red polo shirts bustled about with flakes of hay and buckets.
Others raked and swept. A small dog ran around getting in
everyone's way.

"There's Jen," Holly shrieked.

Their Timber Ridge friend abandoned her wheelbarrow
and ran toward the van. Tufts of auburn hair stuck out from
Jennifer's purple bandana; her Wellington boots glowed with
smears of hoof polish. She stuck her head through the
window.

"About time you guys got here."

Kate promptly forgot all about being cross with Holly and followed her out of the van to hug Jennifer. Arms intertwined, they spun around until they were too dizzy to stand upright.

"Where's Renegade?" Kate said, feeling breathless.

Holly pulled a pot of yogurt from her knapsack. "I brought him a gift—from the train."

"Cool beans," Jennifer said and took them to Renegade's stall. Sure enough—he was the spitting image of Rebel, right down to the star on his forehead, a mane that went on forever, and two white socks.

Another doppelgänger?

As Renegade lapped up his treat, Kate couldn't help thinking that it was getting a bit weird, all these people and horses who had mirror images in another life. First it was Buccaneer and Magician, then Adam and Nathan—even Angela and Princess Isabel, but to be fair they hadn't actually met the princess yet—and now Jennifer's two chestnut geldings.

"Where's Isabel?" Jennifer said, once Renegade had finished slobbering yogurt down Holly's shirt. "Didn't she come with you?"

"Do you *know* her?" Holly said.

"Yeah, she's a hoot, but—"

Jude interrupted. "Isabel's coming down later today," she said, waving toward the van. "Now, come along girls. Unload your suitcases and we'll get you sorted."

* * *

As usual, Holly claimed the top bunk, which irritated Kate more than it should have. Not that she wanted the top bunk—she didn't—but she'd have liked to be given a choice instead of Holly always nabbing it for herself. There was another set of beds, but that top bunk had been claimed as well.

Kate ripped open her knapsack. "Why didn't you tell me about your name?"

"I don't tell *anyone*," Holly said.

"You told Mac," Kate shot back. "And you don't even know him."

There was an awkward silence. Kate bit her lip. This was ridiculous. They were about to have the best adventure of their lives, and what were they doing? Squabbling over Holly's real name.

"It's . . . it's Gladys," Holly whispered.

No wonder she didn't want to share her passport. "I'm sorry," Kate said trying not to laugh, "but *Gladys*?"

Holly threw a pillow at her. "I *hate* it."

"So whose name is it?" Kate said. Parents didn't usually stick their kids with ugly names unless they belonged to an important relative.

"My father's mother," Holly muttered. "She made such a fuss about it that Mom was afraid she'd have a heart attack if her name wasn't bestowed on her one and only grandchild." Viciously, Holly picked at a hangnail. "My grandmother died when I was six months old."

"What about the other one, Hollister?"

"Mom's maiden name."

"Did it come attached to another fierce grandmother?"

"Oh, yes."

"Well, I think Hollister is kind of cool," Kate said, giving Holly an awkward hug as she hung over the top bunk. But it still hurt that Holly—her best friend in the whole wide world—hadn't told her, and she'd had to find out in a station's parking lot.

"If you ever tell anyone," Holly said, "I will kill you."

The door burst open and Jennifer arrived on a wave of barn perfume—saddle soap, horses, and fresh hay. She threw herself into a beanbag chair and yanked off her boots, then balled up her socks and tossed them onto the top bunk.

"So who's in the bottom one?" Kate said.

Its blanket was in tucked tight; both pillows were puffed up like marshmallows. Kate scanned the room. There was no sign of anyone else's stuff—just her suitcase and Holly's, plus Jennifer's messy top bunk and her cosmetic bag spilling mascara, lip gloss, and eye shadow all over the tallest dresser.

"The princess," Jennifer said. "She asked if she could share and I said yes."

"Cool beans," Holly said.

Jennifer grinned. "You bet."

With a feeling she couldn't quite put her finger on, Kate watched as Holly slid off the top bunk and did a little dance, like she was thrilled to bits about sharing their room with a girl they'd never met who sounded too much like Angela for comfort.

6

HOLLY COULD BARELY CONTAIN her excitement. This was even better than meeting her favorite stars last summer when *Moonlight* was filmed at the barn. Then again, that hadn't worked out quite the way Holly hoped. Tess O'Donnell had snubbed them at the premiere, and Nathan Crane turned out to be a real loser.

Luckily, Kate didn't seem to care.

She'd gone with Mac and Jennifer to fetch Isabel's horse from his trainer's yard near Dartmoor. They'd invited Holly to join them, but much as she wanted to see the wild ponies, she didn't want to miss the princess's arrival.

What would Isabel be like?

Was she impossibly glamorous with designer clothes and flawless makeup? Would she extend a perfectly manicured hand and expect everyone to kiss it? Or was she like Rapunzel, Holly's favorite Disney princess, who whacked the hero with a frying pan?

Would Holly be required to curtsey?

Jude was no help. "Isabel's just a girl, like you."

There was nobody else to ask. The other four students hadn't shown up yet, and besides, they probably didn't know Isabel either. Holly chatted with a couple of the grooms. One of them had seen Isabel in a show and said she was positively brilliant; the other sniffed and said it was easy to be brilliant when you had a push-button horse that cost a million pounds.

Holly offered to help muck stalls.

But Jude turned her down. "Take it easy," she said, heading into her office, "because you'll be working hard for the next four weeks."

Feeling restless, Holly watched part of a dressage lesson, then wandered around the stable yard patting noses and dishing out carrots she'd scrounged from the kitchen. According to Jennifer, Beaumont Park owned twenty horses and had ten more in livery, which meant they were boarders. Most of the horses were out in the fields. The rest were in their stalls, except for the six that were in the dressage ring with Nicole Hoffman, one of the Park's instructors and a former Olympic star. There was no sign of Caroline West, Jennifer's famous grandmother.

"She went to Holland this morning," said the cook, rolling out pastry on a heavy wooden table the size of Holly's bed. "To look at some horses."

With nothing else to do, Holly checked out the utility room where they'd be doing their own laundry, then decamped to her bedroom. Maybe she'd practice a few curt-seys. She wobbled left, then right, and finally fell over. Was she even supposed to do this? Americans weren't allowed to pay homage to royalty, were they?

Okay, so how about a stiff little bow—a mere nod—like the doorman at Harrods had given them? Polite, but not fawning. Holly tried a few nods in front of the mirror and felt like a bobble-head. Should she smile or look serious? How about batting her eyelashes? She began to giggle and was doubled over with nervous laughter when Jude knocked on the door.

"Isabel's here. Why don't you give her a hand with her stuff? She's probably—"

Holly didn't need asking twice.

Racing outside, she pelted across the yard. Isabel was getting out of a Range Rover. Holly waved, caught her toe in a rut, and landed face down in the dirt.

Oh, great.

She'd just done the world's most spectacular nosedive in front of a princess and half the grooms at Beaumont Park. She wanted to die.

Like right now.

Better yet, she wanted a great big hole to open up and swallow her. *Kerplunk.* She'd be gone in a flash. Holly rubbed grit from her eyes. Paddock boots with lime green laces swam into view, followed by tanned legs that went on forever and disappeared into frayed denim shorts.

"Are you all right?" said a voice.

Holly scrambled to her feet. "I think so."

"Look, I know the stupid rules say that you're supposed to bow and scrape, but you really didn't need to—"

"Make a fool of myself?"

The girl grinned. "I'm Isabel DuBois, but friends call me Twiggy."

* * *

Instead of driving straight to the trainer's farm, Mac took a detour through the edge of Dartmoor. "We might see ponies," he said. "Or we might not."

Eagerly, Kate peered through the windshield with Jennifer hanging over her shoulder from the back seat.

"Look, there's one."

"Nope, it's just a stump."

Rocky outcrops topped the windswept moors. Mac said they were called "tors" and were part of Britain's largest area of granite. It was wild and beautiful, with patches of dense bracken and scrubby trees . . . and ponies.

Kate saw them first. "Over there."

"Don't feed them," Mac warned, pulling to a halt. "It's not allowed."

"Can I take pictures?"

"Aye."

Carefully, Kate approached the small herd—eight or nine ponies in various shades of brown, bay, and chestnut. One looked like a miniature version of Tapestry with a blond mane and tail. She counted three fluffy foals, but saw no sign of a stallion—just a lead mare who nipped at the other mares' flanks when they got too close to Kate.

She snapped off a dozen photos.

Holly would love this. *Love it.* Why hadn't she come? Why stay behind to meet a snooty princess who probably didn't give a hoot about Dartmoor ponies.

Kate sighed. "I want to bring one home."

"It won't fit in your suitcase," Jennifer said. "Besides, Plug would be totally jealous."

* * *

Wearing a blue monogrammed blanket and blue shipping bandages, Gemini paced his stall as if he were more than ready to leave the trainer's yard. He was a dark bay, just like Ragtime, but his restless behavior reminded Kate more of Angela's old horse Skywalker who used to weave and crib in his stall.

While Mac talked to the head groom about Gemini's feed and hay, Kate wandered toward the outdoor ring. In its far corner a man with spurs and a whip was circling a black horse that looked so much like Magician that Kate did a double take. The gelding's back was rounded, his hind legs engaged, and his nose was so far behind the vertical it almost touched his chest.

Rollkur?

Kate winced. She'd heard people call it "dressage's nasty little word"—extreme flexion of the horse's neck and poll through aggressive force—and it had been banned from competition by the FEI. Gobs of foam covered the gelding's sweaty shoulders; his tail swished like an angry cat.

Jennifer ran up. "Mac says it's time to leave."

"Look at that," Kate said, nodding toward to the horse now being asked to do a passage that he clearly wasn't capable of. Ears pinned, he looked ready to explode. One gigantic buck, and that rider would be toast.

Something about him looked vaguely familiar. Probably his cloth cap. All British horsemen, including Mac, seemed to wear the same ones. But this guy, whoever he was, should've been wearing a helmet.

* * *

The yard was full of horse vans when they got back, except Mac called them horse boxes. Kate was confused. Wasn't that what they called a stall over here?

"No," Jennifer said. "That's a *loose* box."

Kate tucked a few more words into her growing vocabulary. She was determined to get them right and not stick out like a clueless newbie. Mac stopped to let her and Jennifer out and then drove around the back because there wasn't a place to park in front.

Efficiently, the Beaumont Park grooms unloaded the new arrivals—two light bays, a dark brown, and a stunning dappled grey—while four girls in a rainbow of t-shirts, cut-offs, and breeches clustered around Jude who was handing out stall assignments.

"But I want to be next to Margot," said a girl with two

thick braids that reached halfway down her back. Kate wondered how she stuffed all that hair into a riding helmet.

"Me, too," chimed another. She had frizzy red hair and a pointy nose. "Margot's my *very* best friend."

"No, she's *mine*," said the first girl.

They glared at one another, then linked arms with Margot and burst into high-pitched giggles. The fourth girl shrugged. With her sandy brown curls and friendly smile, she reminded Kate of Sue Piretti, Brad's sister. For a split second Kate wished she were back at Timber Ridge and not about to spend the next month with three girls who behaved as if the world owed them a living. Four, if you counted the princess.

Had she arrived yet? And where was Holly?

"Enough," Jude said. "Now, your horses will be stiff, so walk them out before you put them away"—she paused— "in the stalls I've assigned you. No arguments."

Margot gave a little pout and tossed a wave of coal black hair over one shoulder. Any minute now, Kate thought, and she'd be stamping her expensively shod foot. She wore Ariat field boots—French calf leather and full-length zippers—that cost nine hundred dollars. Kate knew this because she'd drooled over the exact same pair at Winfield Tack.

Behind her, Jennifer said, "My gran's going to have her hands full with this lot."

"So why did she choose them?"

"Because they're good riders," Jennifer said.

But the only one who looked comfortable leading her horse around the yard was the girl who reminded Kate of Brad's sister. "What's her name?"

"Bridget Peale," Jennifer said. "She's Irish."

"And the others?"

"English roses, but they've got a few thorns."

Still pouting, Margot led the gray gelding into his stall. Two doors further down, the pointy nose girl was coaxing her dark brown mare inside. The girl with long braids was stalled across the yard, and Bridget Peale was beside her. They both had light bays, but it didn't seem as if they knew one another.

Jude strode up with her clipboard. "Kate, you'll be riding Polestar. Do you want to see him in action?"

"You bet," Kate said and looked along the row of stalls. Most were empty. "Where is he?"

"In the outdoor school," Jude said. "Let's go."

"School?" Kate said.

"Dressage ring," Jennifer said. "And that, over there"— she pointed toward the indoor arena—"is the covered school."

More terms to remember.

Half running to keep up with Jude, Kate followed her through an arched passageway between the house and stable block, then turned right to walk up a gentle hill. At the top was a standard-sized dressage arena with flower boxes, a small judge's pavilion, and black letters on thick white posts.

Five horses and riders were grouped at the perimeter, all watching a magnificent chestnut gelding that extended across the diagonal with hooves that hardly seemed to touch the ground. His rider sat deep in the saddle, hands and legs barely moving. Was that Nicole Hoffman? The brochure said she was an instructor here.

Kate blinked and looked again.

The horse was now performing a flawless pirouette at the canter. Fourth level? Prix St. Georges?

"Is *that* Polestar?"

"Yes," said Jude. "We call him Parsley, and he's all yours for the next four weeks."

7

WATCHING THE PRINCESS UNPACK her enormous trunk was like celebrating Christmas in a very expensive tack shop. Holly lost count of the sage green, powder blue, and white breeches that Isabel—no, *Twiggy*—unwrapped and stuffed into dresser drawers, along with her ordinary buff ones.

Next came a flurry of leather riding gloves, two helmets, and several pairs of boots that must've cost a small fortune. One pair was scuffed with dusty creases at the ankles; another pair was brand-new, judging from the total lack of dirt.

In their bedroom's tiny closet, Twiggy hung up a dozen white and pastel shirts, still with their tags attached. Some had stocks; others had solid-colored ties with gold pins tucked beneath starched collars.

"No ratcatchers?" Holly said.

Twiggy plunged back into her trunk and pulled out a couple of crumpled dresses. She tossed them to one side, then held up a green-and-brown tweed jacket with double slits up the back. "Here it is."

"That's a hunt jacket," Holly said. "Not a ratcatcher."

"Oh?" Twiggy said, raising one perfectly plucked eyebrow. "So what's *your* ratcatcher, then? The Pied Piper of Hamlin?"

"Shirts with stand-up collars." Holly clutched her throat and pretended to gag. "Supertight."

"Cor blimey," Twiggy said in a perfect Cockney accent. "That's so the rats can't crawl down yer neck, innit?"

Holly collapsed in a fit of giggles. Jennifer was absolutely right. The princess was a hoot and nothing like Holly had expected. She'd even apologized for being rude on the phone after Jude had cut her off by mistake.

"I was a bit freaked out over Steffan."

"Your bodyguard?"

"Yeah, but he's okay," Twiggy said. "It took him down a few pegs, though. Big fellow like that being scared of the Eye."

Holly decided not to admit her own fear. "Why didn't he come to Beaumont Park with you?"

"Because I convinced my father I didn't need a bodyguard in Cornwall," Twiggy said, rolling her blue eyes the way Holly did.

It was almost like looking in a mirror. They were pretty much the same height and had the same streaky blond hair, except Twiggy's was a bit more curly. They even had matching toenails. Well, that was because Holly had already shared her favorite nail polish—Plum Crazy—with Twiggy.

"I can give us a French manicure," Twiggy said, showing off elegant hands that didn't look as if they'd ever groomed a horse, never mind wielded a broom or a muck bucket.

Holly swallowed hard.

This was amazing—beyond amazing—all the way into outer space. This morning she'd been nervous about meeting a real live princess—and now, here they were, swapping nail polish and about to share a French manicure. Holly had never had one.

She said, "Can we do it now?"

"Sure," Twiggy said, as the door banged open.

* * *

"Holly, you won't believe the horse I'm gonna—" The words died in Kate's throat.

The room felt different.

Something bigger than both of them had taken it over and was now sitting on the floor beside Holly amid crumpled dresses and a rash of nail polish bottles.

Isabel?

Holly introduced them, but for some silly reason Kate couldn't begin to explain, she had a problem calling the princess Twiggy. Maybe it was Holly's goofy expression or Isabel's offhand explanation. Her family name was DuBois, she said, so everyone had a nickname that related to trees.

"*DuBois* is French for 'of the woods,'" Isabel went on. "My grandfather is Woody, my dad's called Root—but he doesn't use it—and I'm—"

"Twiggy," Kate said. "So, who's Bark?"

"My grandmother's miniature poodle." Isabel yawned, then stretched out her fingers like a cat flexing its claws. She shot Kate a look. "Why don't you like me?"

"Because your horse arrived an hour ago," Kate said, twisting her bracelet. "And you're in here playing with nail polish."

She managed to make her voice polite, almost warm, but inside she was seething. How could anyone ignore a fabulous horse like Gemini who obviously needed a lot more attention than he'd been getting at his trainer's yard?

"So what?" Isabel said. "The grooms will take care of him."

"That's *your* job," Kate snapped.

A strange look wafted across Isabel's face but was gone in a flash. Lazily, she stood up and tapped Holly's head. "I'll see you later."

The moment their door closed behind Isabel, Holly rounded on Kate. "Why were you so mean to her? What did she do to you?"

"She—" Kate bit her lip. The answer was . . . nothing. *Nothing at all.*

The princess hadn't done a thing except hang out with Holly, ignore her horse, and fill Kate's head with idiotic jealousy. She'd never had a best friend before, and now that someone else was moving in on her turf—and fast—Kate didn't know how to cope.

Just like Nathan and Brad.

She hadn't known how to cope with them, either. Somewhere along the line Kate had missed the lessons about best friends and boyfriends that everyone else seemed to have gotten an A-plus on.

Maybe, if Mom were still alive, they'd have sat on the couch with hot chocolate and popcorn, and Kate would've asked awkward questions like "What do you do when your best friend crushes on someone else?" and "Why do I say all the wrong things when boys talk to me?"

But Mom was gone, and Dad had spent most of his life chasing butterflies in Brazil. Kate risked a quick glance at Holly. This was her best friend, the girl she wanted to be sisters with. So why was she, Kate, being such a selfish idiot?

A shiver went through her.

It was warm inside the room, but her feet had turned suddenly ice cold. She wiggled her toes. That didn't help. Maybe her boots were too tight . . . or her heart was.

"For your information," Holly said, looming over Kate like a tornado, "Twiggy is one of the nicest girls I've ever met."

"I'm sorry," Kate said.

But it was too late. Holly gave a dramatic sniff, then turned on her heel and stormed out the door. She slammed it so hard that the hinges rattled.

* * *

At four o'clock, Jude called a meeting in the common room. Most of her students were sprawled across chairs and couches. Kate sat on the floor, eyes glued to a muted flatscreen TV that played three-day-event videos. One of her favorites, Ineke Van Klees, was riding the cross-country course. Next up was—

Jude clicked a remote. "Do I have everyone's attention?"

"Yes," said Bridget Peale.

One by one, Jude rattled off names and told the girls to introduce themselves. "Stand up and speak clearly," she said. "And tell us your horse's name as well."

Jennifer went first. Then came Bridget with Toffee Twist, followed by Margot St. Claire whose dappled grey—Oberon—had caught Kate's attention.

"I'm Zoe Lombard," said the next girl, the one with long braids. "My horse is called Muffin, but that's just his stable name." She paused for a moment. "His real name is Prince Charming, but don't tell him that."

Everyone giggled, and then the pointy-nosed girl chimed in. "Harriet Fitz-Carrington, and I ride Celeste." Sitting down abruptly, she blushed and Kate felt a frisson of sympathy. Blushing was bad enough; it was ten times worse when you had red hair.

The princess had no problem.

"You've probably heard all kinds of dumb stuff about me, but don't believe a word of it," she said, grinning. "My real name is Isabel DuBois, but call me Twiggy, okay?"

"What's your horse's name?" said Bridget.

Isabel's grin faded. "Gemini."

"Doesn't he have a nickname?" Margot said.

"No."

"But you do," Zoe said. She nudged Margot. "How funny."

"I'm Holly Chapman," Holly butted in, as if to cover for

Isabel's awkwardness. "My horse is called Magician, and he doesn't have a nickname either. He's back home in Vermont, and I don't know who I'll be riding here." Expectantly, she looked at Jude.

"Sir Galahad," she said. "He's bulletproof, but for some silly reason we call him Spud."

Holly clapped. "Oh, sweet."

"Potato?" Jennifer said.

After another round of giggles, all eyes except Holly's turned toward Kate. Feeling awkward, she stood. "I'm Kate McGregor, and I'll be riding Polestar—also known as Parsley—because my horse is in Vermont, too."

"Cowboys," Margot whispered to Zoe, loud enough for everyone to hear.

Jude cleared her throat. "The reason you're all here is because you're good riders and you've done well in shows, but after a month at Beaumont Park, you'll be better horsewomen, too. It's going to be hard work. In addition to riding twice a day, you'll be working with our farrier and the vet, plus cleaning tack and mucking—"

"Nuh-uh," Zoe Lombard said, shaking her head so violently her braids flew about. "We have grooms for that."

"Not here," Jude said.

Margot scowled. "So what about all those people wearing red shirts in the yard, then?" She waved toward an open window. "They look like grooms to me."

"You may ask them for advice if you're not sure how to do something, but you'll be taking care of your own horses."

As Jude outlined their stable duties, Kate stared at Margot, Harriet, and Zoe. From the girls' horrified expressions, it didn't look as if they'd ever groomed a horse or saddled one up, never mind mucked a stall. She wanted to laugh about this with Holly, but her best friend was across the room sharing a private joke with Isabel.

Had *she* ever mucked a stall, scrubbed water buckets, or sat up all night with a colicky pony? Kate's cell phone buzzed—a text from Brad. She'd sent him the Dartmoor photos earlier.

Great pix. Tapestry loves them.

A wave of homesickness hit Kate so hard, she gasped. She closed her eyes and could see the Timber Ridge barn— Sue cleaning tack, Robin sweeping the aisle, and Liz giving lessons on Marmalade and Daisy, while Magician and Tapestry stood nose-to-tail in the back paddock swishing flies off one another.

Best friends.

"Are you all right?" Bridget said.

"Yeah." Kate swallowed hard. "Just tired."

"It's jetlag," Bridget said, looking sympathetic. "My dad gets it when he comes home from a business trip to New York. He says it's worse flying east than flying west, but I wouldn't know. I've never been to America. What's it like?"

8

As LUCK WOULD HAVE IT, Spud and Gemini were in adjacent stalls on the other side of the yard from Parsley, which meant Holly had less risk of running into Kate at "morning stables." That's what they called it here. Last night, when they checked on their horses at dusk, it was called "evening stables."

"Sounds logical," Kate had said.

Holly shrugged. "I guess."

They'd avoided one another at supper—eaten on trays in the common room because Caroline West was still in Holland. Jennifer said that when her grandmother got back, she would invite only two or three girls at a time to join her for dinner in the formal dining room, which meant they wouldn't have to dress up every single night.

Kate was probably relieved.

But Holly didn't know for sure. A mask had come down

on Kate's face and whenever Holly looked at her, Kate looked the other way. Already, the eight girls had split into groups. Margot, Harriet, and Zoe stuck together like candy-colored Velcro, while Kate and Bridget had paired off the way Holly and Twiggy had, with Jennifer as a roving ambassador who was friendly with everyone the way she always was.

Holly yawned. Her watch said it was six-thirty, but for her body clock it was still the middle of the night. Bleary eyed and decidedly jetlagged, she ran a hand over Spud's glossy black coat. He yanked his head from the feed bucket to nuzzle Holly's pockets and got bits of grain all over her hoodie, the way Magician always did.

She kissed his velvety nose.

Jude said he loved to jump but was a bit on the stiff side when it came to flat work and that was something they'd be working on with Nicole.

Their lesson began at nine, which gave them just enough time to clean stalls, swallow a quick breakfast, and groom and tack up their horses—a routine Holly could do with her eyes closed. She snagged a couple of empty muck buckets and two pitchforks for her and Twiggy, but when she got back to their stalls, Gemini's door was closed with his rump pressed firmly against it. Holly peeked through the bars.

"Are you okay?"

"Yes."

"I brought you a muck bucket."

"Thanks."

Holly propped Twiggy's pitchfork against the outside

wall, along with the muck bucket, and got busy cleaning Spud's stall. It took less than five minutes. She dragged her half-full muck bucket outside, wondering where to dump it. Twiggy's bucket was still empty, right where Holly had left it.

"Help," said a small voice.

Twiggy?

Holly slid back Gemini's stall door. Its well-oiled rollers didn't even squeak. "What's wrong?"

Twiggy emerged from the gloom clutching a pitchfork. Gemini's bedding looked as if it had been through a meat grinder. So did Twiggy. Her blotchy face was streaked with tears.

She said, "I can't do this."

"Why not?"

"Because I don't know how."

* * *

Kate swung herself into Parsley's saddle. He jigged about while she adjusted her stirrups, then settled down into a flat-footed walk. Almost immediately, he was on the bit.

Jennifer rode up beside her. "Nice."

"But I didn't *do* anything," Kate said.

And she hadn't. It was like that magical moment when Kate was seven and she'd finally learned to post. All of a sudden, everything had clicked into place without any effort on her part.

"Don't get too comfortable," Jude said, climbing into her golf cart. "He can be a beast."

As if to prove a point, Parsley tucked his head and threw

a tiny buck. Kate landed on his neck. Blushing madly, she hauled herself back.

Margot snickered. "Ride 'em, cowboy."

The eight riders followed Jude's cart up the hill and into the outdoor school where Nicole Hoffman introduced herself and said they'd be going back to basics.

And she wasn't kidding. First up were the exercises—bending, touching toes, stretching, and turning in the saddle. No stirrups, no reins; breathe in slowly and then breathe out.

"Remember," Nicole said, walking from one rider to the next and asking their names, "your horse can feel everything you're doing, and he can see most of it, too." She adjusted Gemini's bit, lengthened Harriet's stirrups, and told Margot that her girth was twisted.

"Please get off and fix it."

Kate could barely contain her excitement. This was Nicole Hoffman, the Olympic rider who'd won a silver medal at the European Championships last year. And she was about to give Kate a dressage lesson?

Around the arena they went, across the diagonal, and in twenty-meter circles—all at a walk—while Nicole stressed the importance of good balance and keeping a supple connection with the horse. "Be flexible, not rigid," she said. "I want to see soft hands."

"This is *bor*-ing," Zoe complained.

Nicole didn't argue. "Yes, it is. But it's crucial, so get on with it."

At the end of an hour Kate was dripping wet. Sweat trickled down her neck and crept between her shoulder blades. She never knew that just walking on a horse could be such hard work. Parsley made it seem effortless, unlike Gemini who swished his tail, just like the black horse Kate had seen at his trainer's yard. Isabel's face was pinched, her body stiff. She looked close to having a serious meltdown.

Was she afraid of her horse?

That didn't make sense. This was a program for talented riders, and they'd all been carefully chosen by Jennifer's grandmother. All the girls except Holly and Kate had paid for the privilege, but maybe Isabel's father had paid even more. Well, whatever it was, she clearly didn't belong.

But moments later, everything changed. Nicole had them swap horses—"Part of being a good horsewoman is being able to ride other people's horses"—and Kate found herself on Gemini, while Holly rode Parsley, and Isabel looked like a different rider on Margot's dappled gray, Oberon, who was clearly push-button.

Gemini wasn't. Maybe he once had been, but his buttons were buried so far down, he'd obviously forgotten them. Kate took a deep breath and let it out. She softened her hands, let go of the tension she'd felt while mounting him, and urged him gently forward.

Just a walk—nothing more.

Ears pinned, Gemini danced sideways, and Kate gave him more rein. They were almost on the buckle. "It's okay, boy," she said, patting his sweaty shoulders. Slowly, he stretched. Down went his head and he fell into a flat-footed walk.

"Good," Nicole said. "Keep him going."

Kate risked a glance at Isabel, but she was having such a good time with Oberon that she wasn't paying any attention to what her own horse was up to.

* * *

Over lunch, Jude announced they wouldn't be doing ring work that afternoon; they'd be going for a hack.

"A *what*?" Holly said.

Jennifer grinned. "A trail ride, hacking out."

But to Holly's ears it sounded like a nerdy kid breaking into your computer system. Somewhere she remembered reading that the United States and England were two countries divided by a common language.

Halter, for instance.

Over here they called it a "headcollar," and trucks were "lorries." Well, the big ones were. That morning, Twiggy said it was a bit chilly, so she'd wear her "jumper."

"Jumper?" Holly said, with visions of Twiggy in a pinafore dress. "We'll be riding horses, not going to kindergarten."

Again, Jennifer had come to the rescue.

"It's a sweater," she said as Twiggy pulled a blue knitted hoodie from her trunk and yanked it over her head. In the end, she hadn't needed it because they'd all sweated bullets in Nicole Hoffman's "walking" lesson.

Twiggy moaned about it, but Holly had actually enjoyed it. Riding Spud was a dream; Parsley was even better. Kate hadn't said a word when they'd all changed horses. Holly hoped she would so that maybe then they could start patching things up, but she'd handed over Parsley's reins, taken Gemini, and studiously ignored both Twiggy and Holly.

"Well, la-di-dah," Twiggy said.

Kate didn't hear—or pretended not to.

* * *

Beaumont Park's land stretched all the way to the sea. As Kate rode through the fields beside Bridget, she forgot about her stupid quarrel with Holly and couldn't wait to ride along the beach. It was private, Jennifer had told them, but her grandmother allowed local fishermen to use it. Tourists and campers used another beach half a mile away called Half Moon Beach.

"Can we go swimming?" Zoe asked.

Nicole shook her head. "Not today. I just wanted to show you where it is, and if you come here again, make sure you've got a buddy. Nobody rides—or swims—alone at Beaumont Park, okay?"

Kate had never ridden a horse into the sea before. Leaning forward, she patted Parsley's neck and wondered how he felt about water. Some horses hated water; others loved it, like Magician, who always wanted to lie down and roll.

Zoe scowled. "But I want to swim now."

"Me, too," Margot said. "I'm wearing a suit, so why not?" She yanked up her t-shirt and revealed an iridescent bikini that matched her eyes. Kate stared at her. Margot had to be wearing colored contacts. Nobody had eyes *that* shade of blue.

"Show-off," Bridget muttered.

Margot shot her a scornful look, then wheeled her horse around to join Zoe and Harriet. They trotted off, following Nicole down the path that led to a crescent-shaped beach. Cliffs towered on both sides. Overhead, seagulls swooped and soared, and Kate could hear waves pounding on sand. A wooden sign with peeling paint said *Pirate's Cove*. Just off-shore was a tiny island fringed with jagged rocks and windswept trees.

"What's that?" she said.

Jennifer grinned. "Smuggler's Island."

"How far is it?"

"You can walk out there at low tide," Jennifer said. "But there's a wicked current and the water comes in fast, so you have to time it just right or you'll get stranded."

"Have you been there?" Holly said.

She'd ridden up with Isabel, but neither one of them looked at Kate. It was almost as if she wasn't even there.

"Yes," Jennifer said. "There are caves and tunnels, and the local fishermen say it's haunted."

A couple of them sat on upturned lobster pots while mending nets. Behind them was a ruined castle with broken turrets and crumbling walls. A herd of sheep grazed nearby, and Kate felt as if she'd just stepped back a hundred years.

"Then let's go," Holly said. "After supper. It doesn't get dark until ten o'clock."

"Can't," Jennifer said. "The tide won't be right."

"How about tomorrow?" Kate glanced at Holly. Maybe they could all go together and get beyond the stupid barriers they'd both thrown up. But Holly wasn't looking at her, she was concentrating on Isabel. A flare of jealousy surged up Kate's throat like lava from a volcano. She swallowed hard. Tonight, she'd try and get Holly by herself, away from the princess.

But Isabel stuck to Holly like chewing gum on a rug. They sat together at dinner and giggled over a dumb movie in the common room before traipsing off, arm-in-arm, to the bathroom. As they left, Kate noticed something familiar on Twiggy's wrist.

Holly's special bracelet?

Angrily, Kate twisted her own. They'd both promised one another that they'd never give these bracelets to anyone else. This was getting beyond ridiculous. It was like Holly had lost her own identity and submerged herself in Isabel's life.

Then came the final straw.

Amid even more giggles, Holly gave Isabel one of her stuffed ponies to cuddle in bed because Isabel complained that she'd left hers at home by mistake.

Kate wanted to throw up.

She rolled onto her stomach and pressed her face into the pillow, but sleep wouldn't come. This exciting adventure that she and Holly had been looking forward to for almost a whole year was turning into a disaster.

9

KATE WAS STILL FAST ASLEEP when Holly climbed out of bed. That was odd. Kate was usually awake and raring to go before Holly even had her eyes open. She looked at Kate's face, pale against her pillow, and felt a pang of guilt. Their dumb fight had gotten out of control. Without thinking twice, Holly snatched up her stuffed pony and tucked it into Kate's arms.

"Why are you doing that?" Twiggy said.

Holly paused. "Because."

She'd loaned it to Kate once before when Kate had moved out of Holly's house and into the cottage with her father. She'd also given Kate her spare pony-print comforter, just to make the transition easier. A few months later they'd had a stupid quarrel, over a boy of all things, but managed to patch up their friendship because Aunt Bea had threatened to bang their heads together if they didn't. If only Aunt Bea

74

were here now. She'd have this whole mess sorted out in less than five seconds.

"Hurry up," Twiggy said. "Let's get the bathroom first."

Grabbing a towel and her toothbrush, Holly trundled down the hall after Twiggy. Doors opened and closed. Girls with bleary eyes grumbled about having to get up so early.

Margot yawned. "What's for breakfast?"

"Hay and bran mash," Holly snapped.

Twiggy burst out laughing and dragged Holly into the communal bathroom. But Holly wasn't laughing; she was thinking about Kate and wondering if she'd woken up and found the pony.

* * *

Something soft tickled Kate's cheek. She turned toward it, opened one eye, and let out a muffled shriek.

Holly's pony?

What was it doing here? Had she dropped it, or—?

No, it was a fluffy olive branch. Kate hugged the pony so hard it almost squeaked, and she was still hugging it when Holly returned.

Alone.

"Hi," she said. "You're awake."

"I guess," Kate said. It felt almost odd to be talking to Holly like this. "Look, I'm sorry, and—"

"So am I," Holly said, throwing herself onto the end of Kate's bed. She took the pony, cuddled it, and thrust it back to Kate. "Truce?"

"How about friends?"

"Yeah, that, too." Holly paused. "Just one thing."

"What?"

"Be nice to Twiggy. Please."

"I'll try," Kate said, but it wouldn't be easy.

"She needs our help," Holly said. She snatched her breeches off the floor and climbed into them.

"Why?" Kate said, then found herself not really surprised when Holly explained how Twiggy had never been required to groom her horse or muck his stall or do much of anything around a stable. "She's scared of Gemini, isn't she?"

"I think so," Holly said. "But I can't figure out why."

"I can," Kate said, and was about to tell Holly about Isabel's trainer, when Jennifer and the princess clattered back into the room.

"Let's talk later," Holly whispered.

Kate sighed with relief. "Deal."

* * *

They finally met Jennifer's grandmother at breakfast. Even though Jude towered above her, you could tell they were sisters—the same friendly smile and sparkling gray eyes. Between them stood a boy with wavy brown hair, high cheekbones, and eyes even bluer than the contact lenses Margot had worn yesterday.

"This is Leopold Zeller," said Caroline West. "He came home with me from Holland and he'll be joining our program."

There was an audible gasp from several girls. Even Kate

caught her breath. Leopold was the most gorgeous guy she'd ever seen.

He gave a curt nod, but he didn't smile.

"He's hot," Holly said.

Twiggy sighed. "He's mine, all mine."

"Dream on," Kate said. "Take a look at Margot."

This morning her eyes were jade green beneath lashes heavy with mascara, and right now they were boring into Leopold. But they turned toward Caroline when she beckoned Kate, Holly, and Twiggy over.

"Join me for dinner tonight," Caroline said, "with Jennifer and Leo."

"Watch your back," Kate warned as Margot shot Twiggy a murderous look.

But Twiggy wasn't listening. She was making serious eye contact with Leo, who actually smiled at her. His aquiline nose looked as if it had been carved from marble.

"Score one for Twig," Holly whispered.

They left her talking to Caroline and Leo and headed out to the yard, where Kate filled Holly in on Twiggy's trainer. "He had that poor horse on such a tight rein, it could barely move."

"Rollkur?" Holly said.

"Definitely."

"Well, that won't happen here," Holly said. "You should've heard Nicole railing against it yesterday. She called it an abomination and said that we'd be expelled if we even thought about trying it."

"I don't even know how," Kate said, shuddering. "What

are we doing this morning?" She hadn't felt like checking the schedule because until a couple of hours ago, she'd even considered going home to Vermont. But now that she and Holly were back on track, her enthusiasm had returned in full force.

"Jumping."

"With Nicole?"

"Will Hunter."

"Wow," Kate said. He was another of her favorites. He'd trained at Beaumont Park along with Nicole and Ineke Van Klees.

"And tomorrow," Holly said as Twiggy and Jennifer ran up to join them, "Jude will teach us to gallop bareback, standing up."

"Crikey!" Twiggy said. "That sounds—"

"Like a cowboy?" Kate said.

Twiggy grinned. "I bet Margot will *love* it."

There wasn't room for everyone in the small tack room the students were using, so Holly, Kate, and Twiggy sat outside on two bales of hay with a bucket of water and cleaned their bridles while Jennifer soaped her saddle. Behind them Kate could hear Margot and Harriet complaining. But Twiggy didn't. It was obvious she'd never cleaned a bridle before and had no clue how to remove the reins from Gemini's snaffle.

"Need help?" Kate said.

Twiggy shook her head. "Thanks, but I've got to learn how to do it myself."

"Here," Kate said giving her a bar of saddle soap and a

sponge. "Clean the pieces with water first, then rub the soap in."

"Use this, too." Holly handed Twiggy a toothpick.

She put a hand to her mouth. "Do I have spinach on my teeth?"

"No, it's to poke soap from the holes in your bridle," Kate said.

Twiggy wound up with more saddle soap on her shirt than on the bridle, but she didn't seem the least bit fazed. "It'll wash out," she said airily. "But you'll have to show me how to use the washing machine, okay?"

"Sure," Kate said.

Reluctantly, she had to admit that despite being a spoiled princess, Isabel DuBois was pretty cool. Unlike the other girls, she'd gotten on with cleaning her bridle even though she made a complete mess of putting it back together again and Holly had to sort it out for her.

"*Told* you," Holly said as they rode toward the covered school where today's lesson would be held. At the door, Kate could see Jude on her golf cart talking to a tall man in field boots and dark brown breeches.

Will Hunter?

He was whippet thin and wearing the same sort of cap that Mac and Twiggy's trainer wore. His tanned faced spoke of many hours in the sun. "We'll be attending a show this weekend," Will said to the riders once they were all inside. The only one missing was the new kid, Leo Zeller.

Harriet gasped. "Competing?"

"No, just watching," Will said. "You can learn a lot by

studying the experts." He looked from one girl to the next. "Jumping isn't just a physical sport. It's also mental and emotional."

Kate rubbed Parsley's neck. The chestnut gelding was on edge and eyeing the colorful jumps spread out across the arena. Some were about three-and-a-half feet high, except Jennifer had already warned them that jumps were measured in meters over here.

Along one long wall was a jumping lane—simple verticals with one or two strides between and a continuous side rail, which meant there was no way for the horse to run out. Kate had seen black-and-white photos in the common room of a much younger Caroline West jumping a similar lane with her arms folded—no stirrups, no reins.

"To be really supple," Will said, "you must ride as if you've got ball bearings in your hips."

"Well, that explains it," Jennifer quipped. "Mine are rusty."

"And mine squeak," added Twiggy.

When they'd all finished laughing, Will had them warm up with flat work, followed by several passes over the cavalettis and a low crossrail. At sixteen hands, Parsley was a couple of inches taller than Tapestry but felt much larger. He jumped big, even over poles on the ground, and Kate had a hard time finding her rhythm. She couldn't imagine jumping him without stirrups or reins.

With luck, Will wouldn't ask them to.

* * *

They were twenty minutes into their lesson when Leo showed up riding a dark brown gelding that Kate recognized as Adonis. He was stabled two stalls down from Parsley, and he'd tried to nip her arm earlier that morning when she stopped to pat his nose.

"It figures," Jennifer said in a loud whisper.

Kate looked at her. "What does?"

"An Adonis riding Adonis."

Twiggy gave a wistful sigh as Will said, "I'm glad you could join us, Mr. Zeller, and I trust you'll be on time from now on."

Leo nodded. "Yes, sir."

His voice held a touch of sarcasm, but Will either didn't notice or just let it go. He told Leo to warm up his horse at the end of the arena and join the group in ten minutes. To the girls he said, "When sitting the trot or riding a three-point canter, your seat should stick to the saddle like flies on flypaper."

This roused a few giggles.

"And when you go over a jump," Will went on, "I don't want to see you turn into a praying mantis." Feet apart, he assumed an exaggerated position—elbows tucked and hands perched as if he were a puppy begging for scraps. "Do *not* throw yourself onto the horse's neck. He doesn't want a hug, he wants to get over the jump without you mucking him about."

More giggles erupted.

"You go first," Will said, pointing at Margot. He waved toward a red-and-white oxer that Kate reckoned wasn't much more than two feet. Will was obviously starting them off with the basics, just like Nicole had.

As Oberon cantered toward the jump, Holly said, "What's that in meters?"

"About point six," Jennifer replied.

Holly groaned. "I'll never be able to remember."

Margot cleared the jump easily, but Will criticized her release. "Your hands were too far up the horse's neck," he called out. "You must keep a straight line from your elbow to your horse's mouth."

Scowling, Margot returned to the group. "It's not the way I was taught," she muttered to Zoe. "My trainer likes the crest release."

"And I don't," said Will, whose ears were obviously sharp, "because it makes you unbalanced. But if you want to withdraw from this lesson, I won't stand in your way." He nodded at Twiggy. "Your turn."

Just then, Leo trotted up and flashed Twiggy a devastating smile. Her face turned a delicate shade of pink; she fumbled for her reins.

"Hang in there," Holly said. "You can do it."

Gemini swished his tail. Ears pinned, he bolted forward and Twiggy lost a stirrup.

"Stop!" Will held up a hand. "Pull yourself together. You can't approach a jump like that." He walked up to her and spoke quietly. She nodded and then headed for the jump, but her approach was crooked and Gemini chipped. He barely got over it.

"Poor Twig," Holly said. "She's a mess."

"Yeah," Kate said. "So how did she get into this group?"

Holly leaned toward Kate. "Don't tell anyone, but Twiggy told me that she qualified on her other horse."

"So where is he?"

"Her stupid father sold him, bought Gemini, and stuck Twiggy with a new trainer."

Kate sucked in her breath. "Remind you of anyone?"

"Angela?"

"Yeah," Kate said.

Last summer Mrs. Dean had hired a creepy trainer to coach Angela for the Labor Day show. Angela was scared stiff of him—they all were—but to make matters worse, Mrs. Dean sold Skywalker a few months later and bought another horse without telling Angela.

Just like Twiggy's father had done.

Kate didn't often feel sorry for Angela, but when she'd broken down at the last show, Kate tried to help. In a flood of tears, Angela had confessed that she never dared to form a bond with a horse because the minute she did, her mother sold it and bought a more expensive one. She'd also begged Kate not to tell anyone.

And she hadn't. Not even Holly.

10

DINNER WITH JENNIFER'S GRANDMOTHER wasn't nearly the fancy event that Kate had feared. Nobody dressed up, not even Caroline, who looked comfortably casual in sandals, a long jeans skirt, and a pale pink shirt with a pretty scarf draped around her neck.

"Tell me about your lessons," she said.

For a moment, nobody spoke as if they were afraid to say the wrong thing. Finally, Leo said, "Well, they're rather easy."

Kate almost choked on her soup.

They might have only walked and done a little trotting with Nicole and jumped barely more than two feet in Will's lesson that morning, but the workouts were anything *but* easy. Zoe's horse had trashed the parallel bars, and Adonis had knocked down several rails because Leo wasn't paying attention. He was too busy trying to impress Twiggy.

Like right now.

Across the table he was showing off his custom-made Swiss army knife. "It has a hoofpick, see?"

His voice had no trace of an accent, but his words were precise, clipped even. He sounded like a European trying very hard to be English.

"Amazing," Twiggy said, clearly impressed.

It was odd how Leo had latched onto her. Yes, she was pretty and great fun, but Margot and Zoe were far more glamorous, like the teen models in Holly's magazines. Maybe Leo was impressed with Twiggy's title, not that she used it.

Princess Isabel, Kate decided, was one of the most down-to-earth girls she'd ever met. No wonder Holly had liked her right away. Now all they had to do was teach Twiggy to muck stalls and help her get over being afraid of Gemini.

* * *

On Friday, after a rigorous dressage session with Nicole, Jennifer announced that the tide would be perfect for a trip to Smuggler's Island. She invited Kate, Holly, and Twiggy to go with her. Twiggy wanted Leo to come, too, but Jennifer shook her head.

"Just us girls, okay?"

"What about Bridget?" Holly said. "Let's ask her as well."

"I already did," Jennifer replied. "But she's got a private lesson with Will at three."

"Lucky girl," Kate said. "Are we riding or walking?"

"Riding," Jennifer said. "Jude's given us the go-ahead, so we'll wear bathing suits and find some nylon bridles that won't matter if they get wet." She pulled a bright orange bikini from her trunk. "I'm going bareback."

"Me, too," Holly said.

But Twiggy looked doubtful. "I've never ridden without a saddle before."

Kate was about to say it was no big deal, then changed her mind. That wouldn't help Twiggy. She said, "I'm not riding bareback, either." Then again, she could always take Parsley's saddle off when they got to the beach.

From her knapsack, Holly produced a bag of cookies and four apples. "We'll have a picnic."

"Where'd you get those?" Kate asked.

Holly grinned. "I have friends in the kitchen."

They set off for the beach. Feeling overdressed in jeans and paddock boots, Kate rode beside Twiggy. Ahead were Jennifer and Holly wearing bathing suits and sneakers, which looked kind of odd with their riding helmets.

Pirate's Cove was deserted, no sign of the fishermen. Back home in New England you weren't allowed to ride horses on the beach in summer—too many tourists and vigilant lifeguards—plus they had signs prohibiting dogs, barbecues, and inflatable toys. Here there was nothing except towering cliffs, seagulls, and silvery sand that seemed to go on forever.

"Race you," Jennifer cried.

She cantered Renegade into the surf with Holly and Spud right behind her. Amid screams and giggles, they splashed and jumped the waves. Holly fell off but had no trouble vaulting back on again because the water made her buoyant. The horses began to swim.

"Come in. It's fabulous," Holly yelled.

Twiggy sighed. "That looks like fun."

"It is." Kate hesitated. "Do you want to try?"

"I'll never get on Gemini's back."

"No problem," Kate said. "I'll give you a leg-up."

"Okay," Twiggy said, sounding doubtful. "But how will you get on?"

"I'll manage." Kate jumped off Parsley and removed his saddle. She had no problems vaulting onto Tapestry or even Magician, but Parsley's extra inches might be a challenge. If so, she'd either use a rock as a mounting block or take him into the water and jump onto him there—that is, if he didn't freak out over the waves.

If only Tapestry were here.

Better yet, Magician. He would *so* love this place.

More rocks were exposed because the tide was all the way out and Kate caught occasional glimpses of the sand bar that led to Smuggler's Island. She wanted to canter Parsley across the beach, but Twiggy wasn't ready for that, so they walked and jogged, bending around barnacle-covered boulders and splashing through tide pools filled with hermit crabs and tiny, darting fish.

"How does it feel?" Kate said.

Twiggy wound her fingers through Gemini's mane. He was up on his twinkle toes, snorting and eyeing the waves with his tail flagged like an Arabian stallion.

"A bit wobbly," she said. "Thanks for sticking with me."

Holly and Jennifer met them half way. Both horses were dripping wet. Spud shook himself and showered Kate with cold water—a welcome relief from the sun blazing down from a clear blue sky.

"Love your tankini," Holly said.

"Mine?" Kate said.

"Twiggy's, you idiot."

It was bright pink and covered with silver unicorns, so no wonder Holly loved it. Kate grinned at her. "Help me buy another bathing suit?" she said, hiking up the straps of her ratty old one. Its elastic was about to fail. "This one's falling apart."

"It already did," Holly said, laughing. "You've got a hole in your butt."

Still laughing, she wheeled Spud around and plunged back into the waves. The tide was about to turn, and Jennifer said that if they were going to the island, they'd better do it right now.

"We've got about fifteen minutes," she warned, then followed Holly, who was already urging Spud onto the sand bar. With the late afternoon sunlight glinting off Holly's wet hair and fronds of seaweed clinging to Spud's tail, they reminded Kate of the mystical creatures in Celtic legends about mermaids and kelpies.

She glanced at Twiggy. "Are you up for it?"

"I think so."

Gemini balked, so Kate took his reins and pulled him into the sea, hoping that Parsley wouldn't balk as well. Almost immediately, he began splashing just the way Magician always did. "Don't you dare lie down," Kate said.

Beside her, Twiggy gave a nervous giggle.

* * *

The beach at Smuggler's Island was just like the one at Pirate's Cove, only smaller. And it had caves, so Jennifer had said. Holly looked, but couldn't see any. Maybe they were on the other side of the island. Then, beyond an outcropping of rocks, she spotted a mast swaying from side to side. A ragged black pennant flew from its tip. Skull and crossbones? The Jolly Roger? Holly's imagination ran wild.

"*Pirates*," she whispered.

Jennifer burst out laughing. "It's a sport fisherman. Look, it's got radar and a flying bridge."

"Who owns the island?" Twiggy said.

"It once belonged to Lord Something-or-other," Jennifer replied. "But I think the National Trust bought it about ten years ago."

"So, it's okay for us to be here?" Kate said, sounding worried. "I mean, we're not trespassing, are we?"

"Yes, you are," said a gruff voice.

The man appeared out of nowhere. He wore filthy cargo pants and a *Walking Dead* t-shirt with a pack of cigarettes rolled into one sleeve. Tattoos covered both arms; another crawled up his leg like a serpent.

"Wrong," Jennifer said.

Kicking Renegade, she rode toward him. Fear flashed across the man's bearded face. He stepped backward and tripped over a rock. Down he went.

"Git off my island," he yelled, shaking his fist at Jennifer. "Now. Before I call the police."

Renegade reared and struck out, and for a mad moment, Holly thought Jennifer was going to run the man over. "C'mon, Jen," she said. "Let's go."

The sand bar was almost gone. Waves rolled across it and they'd probably end up having to swim the horses back. Holly told Kate and Twiggy to get moving, then yelled at Jennifer again.

"Hustle."

The man scrambled to his feet. With an almighty roar, he lunged at Renegade, hands reaching for the reins. But Jennifer snatched them free and tore after the others. They splashed across the sand bar—now totally submerged—and plunged into deep-blue water. The horses didn't even hesitate. Heads high and legs churning, they swam like Chincoteague ponies, despite a strong current that wanted to wash them out to sea.

Or worse—smash them on the rocks.

"Phew," Jennifer said, the moment they struggled onto dry land. "That was close."

"Who *was* that guy?" Holly said, breathing hard.

She could still hear him, carrying on like a lunatic above the sound of squawking gulls and crashing waves. Suppose he'd actually gotten hold of Renegade, what then? Holly gave a little shudder. But a small and crazy part of her wanted to go back to the island with a flashlight and explore the caves.

Would Kate go with her?

"Dunno," Jennifer said. "He's not from around here, though. And don't tell anyone about this, okay? They'd only stop us from coming to the beach."

"My lips are zipped," Kate said. "They're also frozen."

"Mine, too," Twiggy said, shivering. "If my father found out, he'd yank me back home or send Steffan down here to drive me potty."

Holly promised to keep quiet, too, then slid to the ground. She wrapped her arms around Spud's slippery wet neck and hugged him so hard he grunted. "We owe these guys a bunch of apples," she said. "They just saved our butts."

* * *

The next morning Nicole had them all swap horses again, and this time Margot wound up with Parsley while Kate rode Spud. Gemini gave Holly a few bad moments, then settled down the way he had for Kate.

It happened so fast, Kate never saw it coming. One minute she was trotting around the outdoor school listening to Nicole's instructions about performing a correct shoulder in; the next, Margot was crashing into her. Spud stumbled and then righted himself, but Parsley went down on his knees.

Nicole rushed over. "That was incredibly stupid."

"Sorry," Kate said.

"Not you. Margot." Nicole pulled her off Parsley, who stood there with his right foreleg bent and his hoof barely touching the ground. To Jennifer, she said. "Go and get Mac. Tell him to bring the trailer."

"It wasn't my fault," Margot said.

"Yes, it was," Nicole snapped. "You're suspended, so go back to the yard."

Stamping her foot, Margot pointed at Bridget, riding Oberon along the rail. " I want *my* horse."

"Go," Nicole said. "Right now."

Margot looked ready to argue, but instead she glared at Kate and stalked off. Behind her trailed Zoe and Harriet.

"I guess the lesson's over," Holly said.

Nicole rubbed Parsley's nose. "I'm afraid it is."

* * *

After the vet diagnosed a bowed tendon, Jude sympathized with Kate. "Parsley will be laid up for a while, and I'm sorry, but we don't have a suitable spare horse right now." She put a hand on Kate's shoulder. "My sister's been hoping to buy a couple of new prospects but hasn't found the right ones yet."

"It's not fair," Holly grumbled once they were alone.

"Margot gets to keep on riding while you're stuck without a horse. They should let you ride Oberon."

"He doesn't belong to Beaumont Park," Kate said. "He belongs to Margot, remember?"

Holly scowled. "They ought to send her home."

"Maybe I'll go instead."

"No way," Holly said folding her arms and looking quite fierce. "We'll share Spud."

"Thanks," Kate said, but it wouldn't be the same. This adventure had just turned sour again.

11

IT TOOK TWO BEAUMONT PARK vans and a Range Rover to get everyone to the show, including Jude, Nicole, and Jennifer's grandmother. Will had gone earlier with Mac in the horse box because a couple of his advanced riders were competing.

They drove past the campground at Half Moon Beach, packed with tourists in mobile homes and tents, then turned inland toward Longstone Downs. An hour later, they pulled into the show grounds.

"Wow, this is a big one," Kate said.

Beyond the riding rings was a stone mansion surrounded by stately trees and manicured lawns like something you'd see in a magazine about English country life. Closing her eyes, Kate had a mental image of an old print she'd once seen—huntsmen in pink coats, a pack of hounds, frock-coated gentlemen in top hats, and ladies riding side saddle, all eager to chase a wily fox that would probably outwit them. At least Kate always hoped he would. She absolutely loathed hunting.

"It's what you'd call an A-rated show in the States," Caroline said as she pulled into a massive field and bumped over ruts looking for a place to park. "You'll see some Olympic hopefuls here," she added.

Jennifer turned around and grinned. "My gran trained half of them."

"Hardly," Caroline said. "And stop exaggerating."

Kate leaned forward. Through the van's windshield she could see bunting and balloons and food carts doing a brisk business selling coffee and pastries beneath striped umbrellas. Her stomach rumbled. She'd overslept and after mucking out Parsley's stall and hosing down his injured leg, all she'd had time to eat was half a toasted bagel and two of Holly's peppermint candies.

It felt odd, though, being at a horse show and only being a spectator. Kate longed to be riding and missed Tapestry more than ever. She texted Brad, even though he was probably still asleep.

My horse went lame and I have nothing to ride. :-(

An hour later she got a reply.

Bummer :-O

By then she and Holly had grabbed a couple of sausage

rolls and were on the rail watching a show pony class with Jennifer and Twiggy, who wore oversized sunglasses and a yellow baseball cap.

"Are you in disguise?" Holly said.

Twiggy glanced over her shoulder. "Yes."

"Why?" Kate said, as a dappled gray pony trotted past. His rider wore jodhpurs and garter straps and a determined expression. She couldn't have been much older than eight.

"Major Ponsonby," Twiggy said, tugging down her cap so its brim almost touched her nose. "He owns this estate and he's a friend of my father. If he sees me, I'll get dragged off for lunch."

"What's wrong with that?" Holly said.

Twiggy pulled a face. "Percival Ponsonby is a pompous prat."

"Try saying that ten times in a hurry without stopping," Jennifer said.

Five minutes later they were still giggling when Bridget ran up to tell them that the open jumper class was about to begin in Ring Two.

* * *

On their way across the show grounds, they passed a large white tent with a sign outside the entrance that said, *Horses for Sale—by Appointment Only*. A uniformed official was checking people's IDs before allowing them inside.

"That's where my gran will be," Jennifer said. "She's looking for another event horse."

"Didn't she find anything in Holland?" Kate said.

"Dutch Warmbloods are super hot right now. Everyone's buying them."

"I know," Jennifer said. "But only if you've got tons of spare cash."

Like Mrs. Dean and Twiggy's father.

Kate didn't say it out loud for fear of upsetting Twiggy. Then she wondered what sort of horse Twiggy had owned before Gemini showed up. Well, whatever it was, it obviously impressed Caroline West enough to invite Twiggy to Beaumont Park.

The first rider was just finishing his round when the girls finally reached Ring Two. They took seats in the small grandstand behind Jude and Nicole. One row further down, Zoe and Harriet sat on either side of Margot. With heads bent over iPods and smartphones, none of them paid any attention to what was going on in the ring.

"I thought this was supposed to be a learning experience," Kate said.

Jennifer shrugged. "I guess Margot didn't get the message."

"Who's up next?" Twiggy said.

"It's one of Will's riders, I think." Kate checked her program, then pointed. "Look, he's down there in the collecting ring." Their trainer stood beside a dark grey horse, talking to its rider and giving her boots one final polish.

"That's Blarneystone," Jennifer said. "My grandmother bought him in Ireland as a two-year-old and trained him herself. His rider is Irish, too."

Shading her eyes, Kate studied the course. The jumps

were just over four feet—1.3 meters—with big spreads, awkward combinations, and tight angles. The steward gave a
signal, and Blarneystone cantered into the arena.

"Look," Jennifer said, nudging Bridget. "He's got your
flag on his numnah."

"His *what*?" Holly said.

Jennifer grinned. "Saddle pad."

Boy, Kate thought. *The Brits had weird words for everything.* But when Blarneystone nailed a clear round and Bridget yelled *Erin go bragh* at the top of her lungs, Kate decided
that the Irish did, too.

"I hope they win the blue ribbon," Holly said.

Bridget looked indignant. "No, the red."

"Why?" Kate said. "That's second place."

"Not over here," Jennifer said. "Red is first, blue is
second. And it's a rosette, not a ribbon."

When she was in fifth grade, Kate had read a book about
an English girl and her pony at their first show, and it was
called *The Red Rosette*. Now she understood why.

Next up was a rangy chestnut that had two refusals and
a knockdown, followed by a bay mare whose rider took a
tumble at the triple oxer. The crowd gasped, but the rider
dusted herself off and got back on her horse. Saluting the
judge, she retired to enthusiastic applause.

"Classy," Jennifer said.

Five more riders went, and one got a clear round. By
this time, Will had returned to his seat and was giving the
girls a running commentary on what worked and what

didn't. Not that Margot and her friends were listening. Leo had just joined them, and they were all over him like ants at a picnic.

Kate glanced at Twiggy. Did she care? No, because her eyes weren't on Leo, they were riveted on the next rider.

"That's my trainer," she said. "Mr. King."

A dozen alarms rang in Kate's head.

It couldn't be, could it? King was a common last name. "What's his first name?"

"I don't know," Twiggy said. "I think it begins with *V*."

Kate studied the rider again. He carried a stiff bamboo cane and used his roweled spurs like a Hollywood cowboy. "It's *him*," she whispered to Holly.

"Who?"

"Angela's old trainer," Kate said, spitting out the words.

Holly gasped. "Are you sure?"

"Positive," Kate said. "It's Vincent King."

His real name was Victor Kavanaugh. He'd once been a member of the British show jumping team, but he got himself suspended for abusing his horses. After that he'd moved to the States and reinvented himself as Vincent King, and then been hired by Mrs. Dean. But when Kate and Holly discovered he was zapping Skywalker with electrified jump poles, Liz threw him out of the barn. And yet, here he was—still abusing horses.

Feeling sick, Kate stared at the black gelding, now fighting the bit and tossing his head. Gobs of foam flew from his mouth and stuck to his sweaty shoulders like tiny marshmallows. It was the same horse she'd seen Vincent King riding at his yard when they collected Gemini.

"That poor horse," Holly said.

Kate couldn't take her eyes off him. With his long wavy mane and that funny little crescent-shaped star, he looked disturbingly familiar. She checked his legs—two white socks, one slightly longer than the other, and both on the left-hand side.

"Oh, my god," Kate said, as realization landed with a thud. "It's Buccaneer."

"The movie director's old horse?" Jennifer said.

Kate clenched her fists. She wanted to drag Vincent King off Buccaneer and beat him up with his cane, just like he'd once threatened to do to her. "Yes."

* * *

At the starter's bell, Buccaneer shot through the gate as if his tail were on fire. He sprang over the first three fences like a cat, then almost fell as Vincent King hauled him into a tight turn, far tighter than it needed to be.

This was insane.

"Slow down," Kate said through gritted teeth. They weren't riding against the clock. Next up was the triple combination, and Kate held her breath as Buccaneer veered toward it. His approach was all wrong, not enough momentum. He'd never—

But somehow he did.

Over the double oxer, two strides and over the gate he

went—both clear. Then came the hogsback, and Buccaneer aced that one as well. Four jumps to go, including a ferocious looking wall that only two other horses had cleared.

On a tight rein, Vincent King aimed Buccaneer at the parallel bars, followed by the Liverpool. Vaulting both as if on springs, Buccaneer got yanked into another sharp turn. To keep from falling, he put in an extra stride and corkscrewed himself over the ascending oxer. His hind foot caught the top rail. It rocked in his cups but didn't fall.

"Aahhh," went the crowd. Someone cheered.

From an awkward angle, Buccaneer approached the last jump. Kate could almost feel his rhythm, his amazing power. She'd once ridden him over fences like this. But something wasn't right. In fact, something was very wrong, and Buccaneer knew it. Despite Vincent King's spurs raking his sides, Buccaneer slammed on the brakes and slid into the wall like a ball player stealing home.

Blocks tumbled out, and Kate cringed when one of them banged into Buccaneer's front legs. She knew they were lightweight, like plastic or Styrofoam, but still—

Vincent King raised his stick.

"No!" Kate leaped to her feet.

Holly grabbed her arm. "You can't."

Shaking free of Holly, Kate flew down the steps two at a time. Could she get into the arena? Was there a gate on this side? Yes, but it was guarded by a steward who'd never let her through. Kate grasped the top rail, ready to climb over, and felt a firm hand on her shoulder.

"Stop," Caroline said. "You'll get hurt."

"But I *know* this horse, I've ridden him," Kate said and was about to push Caroline away when Buccaneer took charge. Dropping his head, the horse gave two almighty bucks and sent his rider flying. Then, still bucking and snorting, he roared toward the gate, swerved to avoid a steward, and jumped clean out of the ring. Spectators scattered like chickens.

"Impressive," Caroline murmured.

12

WITHOUT THINKING TWICE, Kate raced after Buccaneer. She knew it was stupid to chase a runaway horse, but if she didn't, someone else might get there first and hand him over to Vincent King.

She would *not* let that happen.

Not after this. That vicious man had just proved he wasn't fit to ride a horse, much less own one. Or maybe he didn't own Buccaneer. Maybe—

No time to think about that now.

Kate forced herself to run faster. Arms pumping, she dodged around kids and ponies and tried not to trip over loose dogs. They seemed to be everywhere, yapping and nipping at her heels. A man with outstretched arms attempted to block Buccaneer's path; another grabbed for his reins. But the black horse didn't even slow down. He rocketed through the crowd, mane and tail flying, as if he could run forever.

Breathing hard, Kate stopped. Beyond the trees she could see Buccaneer galloping toward Major Ponsonby's manicured lawn. Maybe he'd stop for a snack when he reached all that luscious grass.

A snack?

Of course! That's what she needed. Kate searched her pockets in the hopes of finding a few crumbs of sweet feed, a wizened carrot. Anything. Even a bit of paper would do as long as it rustled.

Holly sprinted up. "Want help?"

"Yes," Kate said. "I need something to catch Buccaneer with."

"How about this?" Holly whipped out a pack of peppermints.

Kate slapped her forehead. "Why didn't *I* think of that?"

Last summer when Buccaneer first arrived at Timber Ridge, nobody—not even Liz—could get anywhere near him until Kate discovered he'd do almost anything for a peppermint Life Saver.

And so, armed with a generous supply of candy, Kate had slowly made friends with the difficult horse. She'd schooled him on the flat and over challenging fences, much to the delight of his former owner, Giles Ballantine. When Kate saw Giles at the *Moonlight* premier, she'd asked where Buccaneer had gone, but the movie director shrugged and said he didn't know. He barely remembered his old horse's name.

"Uh, oh," Holly said. "We'd better hustle."

Kate turned to see an angry Vincent King striding toward

them. Behind him was a posse of helpers, some riding golf carts like a battalion of tanks on army maneuvers.

Buccaneer was a dot in the distance.

She'd never catch him in time. What she needed was someone who could delay Vincent King. He'd pay no attention to Holly, and Kate was desperately searching for help when Twiggy ran up.

Breathlessly, she said, "I've told Major Ponsonby."

"Why?"

"Because he owns Buccaneer. He'll keep Mr. King busy while you—" She gave Kate a shove. "Go."

Lungs almost bursting, Kate ran toward the major's immaculate lawn. Did he know about the abuse? Had he turned a blind eye to how his horse was being treated? Just then, Buccaneer looked up.

Softly, she called his name.

Would he remember her? It was almost a year since he'd left Timber Ridge. They all thought he was going out west to the movie director's ranch. They'd even joked about him becoming a film star. "He could play the Black Stallion," Holly had said.

And right now, he looked the part. Ears pricked and tail flagged, Buccaneer trotted in circles, now and then reaching down to snatch a mouthful of grass. Kate slowed to a walk.

"Here, boy," she said, offering the mints.

Maybe he'd smell them. Buccaneer stopped circling. He whinnied and eyed her warily from behind a tangled forelock. Patches of frothy sweat covered his neck and shoulders.

Backing up, he tossed his head, then inched his way forward, neck stretched out, the way he had done at Timber Ridge when he'd been unable to resist the treat. Kate stood perfectly still, except her hand was shaking—just enough to make the peppermints slide off.

Quick as a snake, Buccaneer scooped them off the ground. Kate held out more. This time he came close enough to touch.

Don't rush it. Don't scare him away.

Itching to pat him, Kate held back. Finally, when she could hardly bear the suspense any longer, Buccaneer took another step forward. He vacuumed up the peppermints, then nuzzled her pockets for more. Gently, Kate took his reins.

"Good boy," she said, rubbing his handsome nose.

Now she was close to him, Kate could see that Buccaneer was thinner than he'd been last summer. A hint of ribs showed below his saddle, and she was about to undo the girth when someone yelled. Nostrils flaring, Buccaneer jerked up his head. His body quivered, on full alert.

Heart thumping like sneakers in a dryer, Kate turned and found herself face-to-face with the last person she wanted to see. She held up a warning hand. "Don't come any closer."

Vincent King ignored her. "Give him to me."

"Over my dead body," Kate said.

She'd never spoken to a grownup like this before. Her legs trembled; a telltale blush crept up her neck. Feeling anything but brave, Kate swallowed hard and looked defiantly at Vincent King. His dark, suspicious eyes were like raisins; his weather-beaten face had more lines than a piece of crumpled paper.

"Out of my way," he snarled and reached for his bamboo stick, tucked into his boot. "I'm going to teach this horse a lesson he won't forget."

But Buccaneer had other plans. Ears pinned, he sunk his teeth into the trainer's arm.

* * *

Holly arrived with Jennifer and Caroline in time to hear Vincent King threatening to shoot Buccaneer. "He's a menace."

"So are you," Caroline said in icy tones.

She'd been filled in by Holly and Jennifer as they followed the golf carts. At first, she hadn't quite believed them, but Holly managed to convince her. "I was there. I *saw* what happened to Angela, and he's done the same to Twiggy. That's why she's scared of Gemini."

"Stay out of this," the trainer said, glaring at Caroline. He rubbed his arm, but his sleeve wasn't even torn. Obviously Buccaneer hadn't bitten him hard enough. "It's none of your business."

"But it is *mine*," came another voice.

Holly whirled around. This *had* to be Major Ponsonby, if only because Twiggy was right behind him, pulling faces. Besides, who else but a retired British major would wear baggy tweed pants tucked into argyle socks? Nodding at Caroline, the major tipped his bowler hat. Holly had a terrible urge to giggle.

Jennifer leaned toward her grandmother. "You saw Buccaneer jump, and I've seen Kate do flying changes with him," she whispered loud enough for Holly to hear.

A smile flickered across Caroline's face. "What are you trying to tell me?"

"That he'd make a great event horse."

"But is he for sale?"

"No," Vincent King said.

"Yes," boomed the major in a voice that belonged on a parade ground.

Twiggy clapped. "A win for Major Ponsonby."

The major smiled and patted her shoulder, but his smile vanished as he rounded on Vincent King. "You, sir," he said prodding the trainer with his stubby finger, "are getting the sack. Effective immediately."

Sack?

Judging by the major's fierce expression, Holly didn't think they were about to have a sack race or pull bags of grain from a truck. Eyebrows raised, she glanced at Jennifer.

Fired, she mouthed.

Holly shot a look at Twiggy. With luck, her father would give Vincent King the sack as well.

* * *

After Vincent King had stormed off, Kate couldn't stop shaking. She couldn't let go of Buccaneer's reins, either. Her hands had curled into claws around them; her legs had turned into jelly.

"Are you okay?" Holly said.

"Yes . . . um, no," Kate said. "I don't know."

A mix of emotions tumbled around inside her like marbles in a pinball machine—relief, joy, excitement, and fear. Or was it hunger? Kate popped a peppermint into her mouth, then fed the rest to Buccaneer. Just hearing him crunch them made her feel a little better.

"Get on him," Jennifer said. "Show my grandmother what he can do."

"Now?"

"Strike while the iron is hot."

Kate didn't feel strong enough to strike anything. She could barely put one foot in front of the other, never mind haul herself onto Buccaneer's back. "I can't. He belongs to the major, and—"

"He's okay with it," Jennifer said. "I already asked him."

Knowing it was hopeless to argue, Kate bent her knee for a leg-up and landed, none too gracefully, in the saddle. Did it belong to the major or Vincent King? The thought of sitting where he'd just sat gave her the creeps.

All of a sudden, she wanted to ride bareback.

But that was stupid. With her wobbly legs, she wouldn't stay on long enough to impress Caroline or anyone else.

Buccaneer was already warmed up, so after a couple of easy circles, Kate urged him into a working trot. By then, Will, Jude, and Nicole had joined her small audience. As she rode past them, Jude smiled and gave her a thumbs-up, but Will's face was hard to read. He stood beside Caroline, and

Kate knew how much she valued his opinion. If Will didn't think Buccaneer was a solid three-day-event prospect, he wouldn't find a home at Beaumont Park.

* * *

Fingers crossed, Holly watched Kate put Buccaneer through his paces. They were both wiped out, yet managed to pull off a decent half pass, two flying changes, and an extended trot that produced a nod of approval from Will.

If Jen's grandmother bought Buccaneer, it would solve Kate's problem. She'd have a horse to ride. Better yet, they'd know that Buccaneer was safe. Holly's cell phone buzzed—a text from Adam.

I'll be in London on Thursday. You coming?

Holly gave a little sigh. When she and Kate had fallen out over Twiggy and weren't speaking to one another, she'd decided to go. She would take the train to London and have fun with Adam at the *Moonlight* party. At that point, it hadn't mattered if she hurt Kate's feelings, but now it did.

No way could she go, unless Kate agreed to go with her. But that would never happen because Kate couldn't care less about parties, and she cared even less about Nathan Crane. Besides, Holly had nothing to wear, unless she borrowed Kate's blue party dress now lying in a crumpled heap at the bottom of their tiny closet.

13

KATE COLLAPSED LIKE A RAG DOLL the minute her feet hit the ground. Someone—she had no idea who—produced a cooler and threw it over Buccaneer's back. Holly took his reins and began to walk him out. Kate sat on the grass, feeling light-headed.

Had they done okay?

Did Caroline approve or had she decided that Buccaneer wasn't worth bothering with? If so, what next? Would Vincent King—or someone else—make an offer the major couldn't refuse?

Despite being hot and sweaty, Kate shivered.

"You guys did great," Jennifer said, flopping down beside her. "I think Gran's going to buy him."

"Really?" Kate said. "What about Will?"

"He's not for sale."

Trust Jennifer to make her laugh. Kate leaned against her,

and they both fell sideways, giggling like idiots. This was insane. She was making a total fool of herself in front of people she admired, but for once Kate didn't care. All that mattered right now was Buccaneer.

"C'mon," Twiggy said, hauling Kate to her feet. "The major's invited us all to lunch."

"No," Kate said, looking at Buccaneer. Head down and ears at half-mast, he walked beside Holly, quiet as a lamb. "I can't leave him. Suppose Vincent King comes back, or—"

"He wouldn't dare," Caroline said, then assured Kate that Buccaneer would be perfectly safe in the Beaumont Park van with Mac standing guard.

"Did you buy him?" Jennifer said.

Her grandmother smiled. "No, but I'm definitely thinking about it."

* * *

Over lunch in the dining tent, Kate discovered that the major wasn't quite the pompous prat that Twiggy had described. Despite his odd assortment of clothes, the major was charming, but he seemed to know very little about horses. So why had he bought Buccaneer?

It wasn't long before they found out.

"I got the horse for my granddaughter," the major said, tucking into a mound of mashed potatoes smothered in gravy. "But she tells me he's too much for her, and she wants a Welsh pony instead."

"So he's really for sale, then?" Jennifer said.

Major Ponsonby smiled at Caroline. "To the right person, yes."

For a moment, nobody spoke. Kate crossed her fingers and would've crossed her toes as well if she'd had room in her boots. But deep down, she knew it wasn't going to work. Buccaneer would end up with somebody else. Then Jennifer leapt to her feet and banged a spoon on her plate.

Conversation at other tables ceased. Half a dozen amused glances came their way. "Sold," Jennifer announced like an auctioneer, "to the best grandmother in the world"—she looked around the table—"unless there are any other bids."

Somebody cheered. "Well done."

Caroline held up her hands in mock defeat. "Who am I to argue with my granddaughter?"

"Or with me," Will said. "He's a fine horse."

"I second that," said Nicole, winking at Kate.

Caroline turned to her sister. "Is this a conspiracy?"

"No, it's good business," Jude replied. "You need another event horse, and he's just landed in your lap."

"For a song, I might add," said the major.

Holly began to sing *Hey Jude*. Major Ponsonby joined in—totally off key—and everyone burst out laughing.

* * *

Kate sighed with relief as the horse show's vet declared Buccaneer sound—just a little underweight—and the farrier said his feet were in good shape. After that, Caroline and the major trundled off in a golf cart so they could talk money and sign papers at his house.

As far as Kate knew, Buccaneer didn't have a pedigree, so he wouldn't cost nearly as much as a registered Dutch Warmblood. Liz had always believed he was mostly Thoroughbred with a touch of Fresian, which accounted for his glamorous mane. Kate figured he was part kangaroo as well, given the way he'd jumped out of the ring. Clipping a lead rope to Buccaneer's halter, she led him out of the van and let him graze. He gorged on the grass like he'd never had any before.

"He's probably been cooped up in a stall," Holly said. "I bet Vincent King never turned him out."

The others had gone to watch more pony classes, but Holly had stuck around. She seemed restless, as if there was something on her mind that needed talking about.

"Spit it out," Kate said as Buccaneer dragged her toward another patch of grass thick with clover.

"What?"

"Whatever it is that's bugging you."

Holly shoved both hands in her pockets. "It's Adam. He's—"

"Dumped you?" Kate blurted.

To her relief, Holly laughed. "No, silly. Nothing like that."

"Phew." Kate wiped her brow. That would be awful, getting dumped by your boyfriend when you were three thousand miles away.

"He's coming to London on Thursday," Holly went on,

her words tumbling out so fast Kate could barely keep up. "There's a big party and he wants me to go with him."

"That's great," Kate said. Holly adored parties. Any excuse to get dressed up and put on makeup, and—

Wait a minute.

Adam was going to be here, in England? That made absolutely no sense. Nobody in their right mind would fly all this way just for a party, even if they could afford it—which Adam could not. He wasn't one of the rich kids; he worked at his barn to pay for Domino's board, the same way Kate did.

"You're joking, right?" she said.

"No," Holly said. "But I can't go."

Kate decided to play along, even though she didn't believe for a single minute that Adam was actually coming over. "Why not?"

"Because—" Holly deflated like a spent balloon. Her voice cracked and she looked close to tears.

Just then, the others came racing back. Breathlessly, Jennifer said, "You've gotta come and see this. It's *too* cute."

"What is?" Kate said.

"The Shetland ponies," Twiggy said. "They're steeplechasing."

"Wow, that sounds awesome." Holly looked at Kate. "Are you coming?"

"I can't leave Buccaneer on his own."

"Ask Mac to watch him," Jennifer said.

Kate shook her head. "He's gone to lunch."

"Bummer," Twiggy said, grabbing Holly's arm. "C'mon, let's go. We're missing it."

"Take pictures," Kate yelled as they ran off.

Holly's doom and gloom had vanished, and Kate began to wonder if she'd just been pranked. Adam wasn't really coming over. It was Holly playing tricks, and she'd be teasing Kate about it by the time they got back to Beaumont Park.

* * *

They got there just in time for the second race. Kids wearing goggles and brightly colored silks mounted their ponies and lined up, jostling for position. Then down came the starter's flag and they were off, galloping around the arena in a high-speed dash over two-foot brush jumps.

"Wow." Holly's breath came out in a whoosh. "This is fantastic. I bet Plug would love it."

"Dream on," Jennifer said. "He's too lazy."

In the lead was number seven, a girl in pink and blue stripes riding a black Shetland that couldn't have been more than nine hands. Then rider number three fell off, but her pony kept going. Tearing around corners, the tiny chestnut jumped all the fences and wound up in second place.

Holly wanted to hug him. "Will he get a ribbon?"

"They all will," Twiggy said as another group of pony jockeys entered the arena. "I'm betting on number four."

"Two," Jennifer said.

Holly picked number six because he was the smallest and he reminded her of Plug. His rider wore bright red silks with yellow stars, and there was a red pom-pom on top of her yellow helmet cover. Her pony took the lead almost immediately, churning up the ground as fast as his short little legs would carry him. Holly snapped off a bunch of photos and sent one to Adam.

Shetland pony racing!

Number six beat number four by a nose, and Holly was high-fiving with Twiggy when Adam texted back.

Way cute. See you Saturday!

He assumed she was coming, and even though she'd already tried to explain about Kate, he didn't get it. Guys never did. They handled stuff like this differently than girls. A guy would just tell his best friend he was going to a party or whatever, and that would be that. No trauma over hurt feelings.

Holly caught her breath.

She'd gotten herself caught between a rock and a hard place. No matter which way she jumped, someone was going to be mad at her.

* * *

Kate rode back to Beaumont Park behind Mac, squashed into the cab's rear seat with a bale of hay and two saddles. It was as close as she could get to Buccaneer without actually being in the van with him, not for want of asking, though.

"That's not on, lassie," Mac had said. "Ye'll sit up front with me and Will."

While the men discussed the next horse show, Kate closed her eyes and drifted off. In her dream, she was riding

Buccaneer along the beach, jumping rocks and upturned rowboats. They splashed through monstrous waves, going deeper and deeper as they swam toward Smuggler's Island. Through a swirling mist, the pirate ship emerged; the bearded man yelled and waved his tattooed arms.

Then Cornwall morphed into Vermont, and Kate found herself riding Tapestry and telling her about Buccaneer, which turned out to be a really bad idea because Tapestry got all jealous and bucked Kate off.

She woke up with a start.

Mac was already unloading Buccaneer by the time Kate pulled herself together and took over. She removed Buccaneer's blanket and shipping bandages, then led him around the yard while one of the grooms spread fresh bedding in the stall beside Parsley.

"No riding for a couple of days," Caroline said. "He needs to settle in. You can turn him out tomorrow, let him run about for a bit." She patted Buccaneer's shoulder. "I get the feeling this fellow hasn't spent much time outside in the past few months, and I'm counting on you to keep an eye on him."

Kate opened her mouth and promptly shut it again. A simple *thank you* didn't seem quite big enough, and she was still searching for the right words when another horse claimed Caroline's attention. With a knowing smile, she turned away and for some odd reason Kate suddenly felt all grown-up, as if she'd just been trusted with the keys to Caroline's car.

14

HOLLY TRIED TO GET KATE on her own so they could talk about Adam and the party, but people kept interrupting. First it was Bridget, followed by Twiggy, who dragged Leo with her to admire Buccaneer as well. Then came Margot and her two faithful groupies.

"Keep him away from me," she said as Buccaneer stretched out his nose hoping for a treat. Margot took a hurried step backward. "He's dangerous."

"Don't worry," Holly said. "He won't bite you."

Margot narrowed her eyes. "Why not?"

"Because you taste yucky."

"Like Marmite," Kate said.

Holly almost gagged. That morning Twiggy had dared her to try it, so Holly had spread the sticky brown stuff on her hot buttered toast the way all the English girls did. Then she took a bite and almost threw up. Totally revolting. Even worse than liver, and that was bad enough.

Finally, everyone wandered off, and Holly was about to beg Kate to go to London with her, when Will and Nicole showed up.

"Everything all right, then?" Will said.

Kate nodded. "Yes, he's settling in."

As if to prove a point, Buccaneer promptly frisked him for treats. Will laughed, then said, "How about an extra lesson? I have time on Saturday."

"So do I," Nicole said. "We'd both like to help you with Buccaneer."

"Wow," Kate said. "I'd love it. And thank you."

Holly's heart sank. Kate would never give up two private lessons to attend the party in London, no matter how much Holly begged. Feeling glum, she left Kate talking to their instructors and trudged back to her room.

Twiggy lay sprawled in the beanbag chair, gazing at Nathan Crane on the cover of Holly's magazine. "He is *so* dreamy. Don't you just love him?"

"He's okay," Holly said and threw herself onto Kate's bed. "But what about Leo?" Last she knew, Twiggy was madly in love with him. He was all she'd talked about ever since he arrived.

"Pffft," Twiggy said. "Leo's a silly schoolboy compared to Nathan Crane." She gave an elaborate sigh. "I'd give *any*thing to meet him."

Holly sat up so fast, she banged her head on the top

bunk. A plan was starting to take shape, but she'd need Twiggy's help to pull it off. "Okay," she said. "What would you give?"

Twiggy sighed again. "My right arm."

"No need for that," Holly said. "A simple bit of skull-duggery will do just fine."

Skullduggery?

Where on earth had that come from? It made her sound like an amateur sleuth—something straight from the pages of a *Nancy Drew* mystery. Feeling positively clandestine, Holly jumped off the bed and put her ear to the wall. It would be just her rotten luck for Margot to overhear her plan and blab it to Kate. But she heard nothing, not a sound. She flopped down beside Twiggy. "Have you seen *Moonlight*?"

"Like, about three times already."

"Remember the scene where Ophelia Brown is chased by the zombies, and—"

"—Ian Hamilton rescues her?"

"That was Kate and Adam." Holly waited a moment for it to sink in. Twiggy's eyes grew so big they almost popped off her face. "They were stunt doubles for Tess O'Donnell and Nathan Crane. Part of the film was shot at Timber Ridge, and Kate was riding my horse."

"Magician?"

"Yup," Holly said. "And Adam was riding Domino."

For once, Twiggy was speechless. She opened her mouth but nothing came out except for a muffled gasp.

"There's more," Holly said.

"More?" Twiggy croaked.

"Nathan was Kate's boyfriend, but she dumped him."

Twiggy swooned, or something close to it. Her eyes rolled upward and she slumped into the beanbag chair, arms and legs flung wide. Had she fainted? Like for real?

Now what?

Holly rubbed Twiggy's limp hand, then tapped her cheek. What about smelling salts? Did people use those any more? She was about to go for help, when Twiggy opened one eye.

She grinned. "April fool."

"It's July, you idiot," Holly said. "And I wasn't fooling about Kate and Nathan." She took a deep breath. "So, do you want to meet him or not?"

"Are you kidding?" Twiggy said. "When?"

"This Saturday," Holly said, then explained about Adam and Giles Ballantine's big party and how Kate might be hurt if she found out. "She's got two private lessons this weekend, so she wouldn't have come with me anyway. But don't tell her, okay? And don't tell anyone else, either."

"So how do we get away from here?" Twiggy said. "We can't just say, 'We're going to London,' and then toddle off to the station. It's like twenty miles away. Besides, they'd never let us go without permission."

Holly hadn't thought of that. "Any ideas?"

"I'm an expert at this," Twiggy said.

"You are?" Holly said. "Why?"

"Boarding school. I've done a bunk quite a few times."

"Bunk?"

"Escaped," Twiggy said. "Scarpered."

Holly wanted to shake her. "Speak English, and hurry. We don't have much time." The others would be upstairs at any minute to get ready for dinner.

"I'll tell my father there's nothing going on here," Twiggy said, "so I've invited you home for the weekend. He'll e-mail Caroline and send Steffan down with the car on Saturday to pick us up."

"You make it sound easy."

"It is," Twiggy said, "when you've got pots of money."

She pulled a silly face, but underneath Holly detected a hint of bitterness, as if Twiggy resented her wealth. Holly couldn't begin to imagine how it must feel to be enormously rich. It was probably a lot more complicated than most people thought.

"What about the party?" Holly said. "How do we handle that?"

"My parents usually go to the theater or the opera on Saturday nights, so we'll sneak out after they've left."

"Suppose they don't go. What then?"

"No problem," Twiggy said. "I'll just tell them we're going to my cousin's for a sleepover. Claudia will cover for us."

"Where does she live?"

"Two streets over. We can walk there."

It all sounded a bit hairy, deceiving her parents and sneaking about like burglars. But Twiggy said she'd done it before, lots of times, and never been caught.

"Are you sure about this?" Holly said.

"Yes," Twiggy said. "But first you'd better pinch me."

"Why?"

"To prove I'm not dreaming." With a dramatic sigh, Twiggy flopped back into the beanbag chair hugging Holly's magazine. Her eyes fluttered closed as the bedroom door banged open.

"What's up with her?" Jennifer said.

Gently, Holly pinched Twiggy's arm. "She's having a dream, that's all."

"Must be a good one," Jennifer said, kicking off her boots. "She's grinning like an idiot."

* * *

While the others had lessons with Will and Nicole, Kate fussed over Buccaneer like a mother hen. She took him for long walks and introduced him to the other horses. Sometimes, she'd sit in his stall reading a book, and he'd rest his head on her shoulder and give a little sigh as if he were grateful that she'd rescued him. She also discovered that he liked Polos just as much as he liked Life Savers.

"He'll get spoiled," Jude said, feeding him a mint.

"Too late," Kate said. "He already is."

Jude ran her hands over Buccaneer's shiny rump where Kate had been experimenting with quarter marks. "Nice," she said. "I could never get the hang of these." Slowly, she turned toward Kate. "You're going to miss this fellow when you go back, aren't you."

Kate sniffed. "Yeah."

Last summer she'd taken care of Buccaneer, and in those few precious months he'd managed to steal a tiny piece of her heart. Having him back again was like finding buried treasure.

"You're good together," Jude said. "With the right training, this is a horse that could take you far."

After Jude left, Kate tried to dismiss her words as nothing more than idle praise, but they stubbornly refused to leave. They bounced around inside her head like ping-pong balls—all the way through dinner and evening stables. That night, she dreamed about riding Buccaneer in the Olympics, then woke up in a panic, feeling as if she'd just betrayed Tapestry.

* * *

For the next two days it was gray and cold, with spatters of rain being flung about by the wind. When it blew really hard, branches from a low-hanging tree brushed against the covered school's roof and spooked all the horses—except for Spud. Nothing seemed to faze him, not even a plastic bag that tumbled across the arena like a tiny ghost and sent Adonis and Muffin into orbit. Zoe almost fell off, and Leo had a hard time getting his horse's feet back on the ground.

"Pay attention," Nicole said. "We're not here to play games. Now, let's try cantering again. Inside leg on the girth, outside leg behind it. Hold your horses together, stabilize them. Use your seat."

But Holly's mind kept wandering.

Adam flew in later today, and she still hadn't told Kate about the weekend in London. Twiggy's father had already e-mailed Caroline that he'd be sending a car to pick them up early on Saturday morning. By two o'clock, they'd be at

Twiggy's favorite beauty salon; at four-thirty they'd be ransacking Twiggy's walk-in closet for just the right outfits. She had hundreds, apparently.

So, what could possibly go wrong?

The worst would be Kate finding out and never speaking to Holly again. No, that was insane. Kate was so wrapped up in Buccaneer that it was like the rest of the world had ceased to exist. But Holly had to tell her *something*. A half truth would be best. She'd just mention, casually, that Twiggy had invited her to London for—

What?

Museums, art galleries? An opera?

That was crazy. Okay, how about shopping? Kate loathed shopping even more than she loathed parties, and she'd be relieved that Twiggy hadn't invited her as well, so—

"Miss Chapman," said Nicole. "Over here, please."

Margot snickered. "You're in for it now, cowboy."

Pulling her scattered wits together, Holly trotted toward Nicole. She wasn't smiling—a bad sign. Nicole was always cheerful, unless she was bawling somebody out.

"You've been in la-la land for the past five minutes," she said, laying a hand on Holly's boot. "Is something wrong?"

"No," Holly said. "Everything's fine."

Not.

She was about to lie to her best friend, and right now, she felt awful about it.

15

To Kate's relief, Buccaneer remembered most of what he'd learned the previous summer. The trouble was, he also remembered his training with Vincent King and worked himself into a lather whenever Kate asked for collection. To him, it meant pain.

"Horses have amazing memories," Nicole said. "So let's focus on getting his trust back. He needs to know that you won't hurt him or ask him to do anything he's not ready for."

A steady rain hammered the covered school's metal roof. Kate shivered. It was hard to believe she'd been swimming at Pirate's Cove the week before. Tomorrow afternoon, they were going on another beach ride, with a proper picnic this time. But if the rain didn't stop they'd all be huddled beneath umbrellas, eating soggy sandwiches and wishing they'd worn fur-lined breeches instead of bathing suits. Kate still hadn't bought herself a new one.

Jennifer insisted the weather would clear up. "And if it doesn't," she said cheerfully, "who cares? We'll be getting wet anyway."

As Kate trotted Buccaneer in twenty-meter circles, she had visions of riding him along the beach. A gentle breeze would ruffle Buccaneer's mane; the sun would make his ebony coat sparkle. Like a scene from *The Black Stallion*, they'd dance through the surf and jump waves. They'd swim—

Was she completely mad?

One glimpse of water and Buccaneer would totally freak out like he did last summer on the Timber Ridge cross-country course. The stream there was narrow, barely more than a trickle, but it had taken all of Kate's ingenuity—and a pack of Life Savers—to get him over it.

* * *

By noon on Friday, the sun had come out, and everyone signed up for the picnic. Even Jude agreed to come with them. She would bring the food and soft drinks on her golf cart. According to Jennifer the Beaumont Park kitchen had prepared quite a feast—Cornish pasties, sausage rolls, cucumber salad, and flasks of lemonade with a cream tea for dessert.

"Cream tea?" Holly said. "What's that?"

"Scones, clotted cream, and lashings of strawberry jam," Twiggy said, smacking her lips. "Totally yummy."

Kate patted her pocket to make sure she had plenty of Polos to bribe Buccaneer with. She didn't have much hope that he'd go anywhere near the water, but she was wearing her ratty old bathing suit beneath her shorts, just in case.

To her surprise, Buccaneer didn't even balk. He jumped the smaller tide pools and sloshed through the bigger ones, then gave a startled snort as the white froth of a wave broke around his legs. He tried to eat it.

"Wow," Kate said, still in shock. Somehow, Buccaneer had turned from a landlubber into a seafaring pirate. He began to splash—one foreleg, then the other.

"Watch out!" Holly yelled.

In what felt like slow motion, Buccaneer's front end collapsed, and down he went. Kate threw herself off his back, laughing so hard she swallowed a mouthful of salty water.

"See," Holly said. "He's finally figured out what his name means." She pointed toward the faded beach sign. "They should call it *Buccaneer's Cove*."

* * *

As they rode through the surf, Holly casually mentioned that Twiggy had invited her to London.

The tide was coming in and already the sandbar had disappeared. There was no sign of the tattooed man's power boat, either. Holly shuddered. That thing gave her the creeps.

"Are you going?" Kate said.

Holly shrugged. "Yeah, I figured you'd be busy, all tied up with Will and Nicole, and . . ." Her voice trailed off. She wanted to look at Kate to gauge her reaction, but didn't dare for fear of giving the game away.

No, not a game.

She was protecting Kate's feelings. That's what best friends did for each other. But this was a whole lot more difficult than Holly thought it would be, and right now there was an awful silence. Kate was probably putting two and two together and coming up with nine hundred.

"Will Adam be there?" Kate's voice had an edge to it.

Holly crossed her fingers and twisted them into Spud's mane. "I was only kidding."

"What about that big party?"

"I was kidding about that as well," Holly said. A beady-eyed gull waddled toward them. It snatched up a wizened french fry and flew off. Holly wanted to go with it—just fly away and leave her lies on the sand like discarded junk food. "Twiggy and I are getting our hair done, and then we're having a sleepover at her cousin's house."

"Sounds like fun," Kate said. "Let's go for a swim."

With that, she wheeled Buccaneer around and plunged into the waves. Holly had no idea if she believed her or not.

* * *

The others were still fast asleep when Kate crept out of their bedroom. The grooms were already hard at work, so Kate pitched in. She mucked out Buccaneer's stall and then Parsley's. While both horses were eating their grain, she cleaned Buccaneer's tack.

Jude stuck her head around the door. "Hey, you're missing breakfast."

"Not hungry," Kate said, rubbing soap into Buccaneer's

show bridle. Its glitzy, V-shaped browband reminded her of the one Holly had given her for Tapestry last summer.

"Nonsense," Jude said. "You can't ride on an empty stomach. Go and get something to eat. That bridle can wait."

Kate stood up. Her legs were still stiff from riding Buccaneer bareback yesterday. Was Holly awake yet? Had she and Twiggy left for London? Kate didn't really want to see either of them. Last night after supper, she'd gone for a long walk with Bridget, and by the time they got back Holly was already asleep. So was Twiggy, thank goodness.

This was totally childish.

Like off-the-wall childish. But Kate couldn't help herself. She had no interest in going to London—especially shopping and a sleepover with someone she didn't know—but it would've been nice if they'd invited her.

"Hustle," Jude said. "Cook made waffles."

Kate hung Buccaneer's bridle on its peg, shoved her saddle soap into a plastic bag, and was about to head for the house when an enormous black car with tinted windows cruised into the yard.

Princess Isabel's limousine?

It was even bigger than the one Giles Ballantine had provided to take them to the *Moonlight* premiere in New York. Almost immediately, the front door banged open, and Holly raced outside, followed by Twiggy. They skipped down the flagstone path, laughing and squealing like a couple of kids getting out of school early. Neither of them saw Kate standing in the tack room doorway and feeling desperately left out.

For some idiotic reason she couldn't begin to explain, Kate wanted Holly to wave and say, "Hey, come with us." But of course, she didn't, and the car purred off as smoothly and silently as it had arrived.

* * *

Someone had left a copy of *Hello!* on the common room's buffet table. Kate helped herself to waffles, whipped cream, and fresh strawberries, then grabbed the magazine. Its front cover promised an article on Britain's gold medal dressage team, but as Kate flicked through the glossy pages, all she found were pictures of rock stars and celebrities and a few of the more interesting royals. Zara Phillips looked quite dazzling on her latest event horse; Prince Harry had yet another new girlfriend.

Kate took a huge bite of waffle, then turned the page and promptly spat her breakfast all over it. Half a strawberry landed on Nathan Crane's nose; whipped cream added highlights to Tess O'Donnell's golden hair. The caption read:

These Stars Will Shine at the Moonlight Gala in London on Saturday Night

Kate stared at the words, waiting for them to sink in and make sense. How had she missed this? Nathan's face was on billboards and buses all over London. She'd even joked about it with Holly.

Was *this* the big party?

* * *

Kate's dressage lesson started badly and got progressively worse. All she could think about was her best friend, zooming toward London with Twiggy in that outrageous car, sniggering and talking about Kate behind her back. She felt herself stiffen.

So did Buccaneer. Ears pinned, he tossed his head and skittered sideways like a crab. Tightening her reins, Kate glanced at Nicole. She was trying to explain something.

"—ease up with the leg and hands until you need them again."

"Sorry," Kate said. "I missed it."

Nicole sighed and walked over. "Your mind is obviously somewhere else. You're not paying attention. It's like I've been talking to myself for the past ten minutes."

"I'm sorry," Kate said again.

She was blowing this golden opportunity, and she'd never get another. Nicole would probably tell Will to cancel her jumping lesson that afternoon, then Caroline would forbid her to ride Buccaneer. She'd give him to Leo, or—

"Here's what you missed," Nicole said. "Encourage your horse by letting the reward be bigger than the ask. The moment he does what you want, ease up—"

Kate nodded. She knew all this. Liz had drummed it into her, over and over, but right now it seemed as if everything she'd ever learned about riding and communicating with a horse had flown out the window—thanks to Holly's idiotic lies.

No, that wasn't fair.

It wasn't Holly's fault. It was hers. She'd built an invisible wall and hidden behind it, just like she always did whenever feelings were involved. Holly wore hers on her sleeve; Kate's were buried so deep she needed a shovel to dig them out.

Nicole said, "Let's start over."

"Seriously?"

"Yes, seriously." Nicole dug into her pocket and pulled out a Polo mint. "This isn't exactly an approved training aid," she said, feeding it to Buccaneer. "But right now, I believe it will help."

Kate smiled. She felt a little better already.

* * *

With Twiggy's stone-faced bodyguard at the wheel, they drove to London in just over four hours. The ride was so smooth and so comfortable that Holly almost forgot she was inside a car—except when Steffan's disembodied voice wafted through the sound system. Did they need to stop and stretch their legs?

"He means a potty break," Twiggy whispered.

Holly giggled. "I'm cool."

"So is Nathan Crane," Twiggy said and launched into another round of questions about *Moonlight* and what Nathan was really like.

Holly decided on the short version. No sense in bursting Twiggy's bubble—at least, not yet anyway. "He went to school with Adam," she said, choosing her words carefully. "They acted in plays together—musicals and stuff. Then a

talent scout showed up and whisked Tom off to Hollywood."

"Tom?" Twiggy said.

"Woops," Holly said. She hadn't meant for that to slip
out. "Nathan's real name is Tom Smith."

Twiggy's mouth dropped open. "You have got to be kidding."

"Nope," Holly said. "But he keeps it secret, so—"

"My lips are zipped," Twiggy said running a finger
across them. "And don't tell anyone I'm a princess, okay?"

"Too late," Holly said. "Adam already knows."

"Does Nathan?"

"Do you want him to?" Holly said.

Not that Nathan would care. Everywhere he went, girls
swooned and fans begged for his autograph. If you believed
his Twitter page, half the princesses in Europe followed him.

So did the paparazzi.

In Hawaii they'd photographed Nathan punching a
surfer who accused him of stealing his girlfriend; in New
York he'd been videotaped while being dragged out of a
nightclub by his bodyguard. The newspapers said he was
drunk, but Nathan claimed it was food poisoning. Another
time, he'd flown into a temper and busted a fan's camera.
The paparazzi captured that moment as well.

Twiggy shrugged. "I guess."

"So, if you're not a princess tonight," Holly said, pinning
her with a look, "who are you?"

"Isabel Wood," Twiggy said. "Belle for short."

Beauty and the Beast?

Holly crossed her fingers—she'd been doing a lot of that lately—and hoped Adam would keep his best friend in line. It didn't take much provocation from an aggressive reporter for Nathan Crane to morph into a camera-smashing beast.

16

STEFFAN DROPPED THEM AT RICARDO'S, Twiggy's favorite beauty salon. He would be back an hour later to pick them up, but Twiggy told him they would walk home.

"He's only doing his job," Holly said as Steffan drove off looking none too happy.

Twiggy sighed. "I know, but he's a pain in the neck. He's on my case all the time. I can't even take a step in London without him following me about like a—"

"Puppy?" Holly suggested.

Twiggy snorted. "More like a Rottweiler."

The salon's door opened, and within moments Holly found herself wrapped in a silky black cape and sitting in front of a gilt-edged mirror. Soft rock played in the background; her chair was divinely comfortable. This place had to cost a small fortune. Good thing Twiggy had insisted on paying—with her father's credit card, of course.

"Split ends," Ricardo said as he examined Holly's limp hair. She felt acutely embarrassed for not having washed it that morning. "Let's get rid of them, shall we?"

"Don't cut too much off," she said.

He picked up his scissors. "Just a smidge."

Holly had no idea what that meant, but Twiggy had promised that these guys really knew what they were doing. Then came a luxurious shampoo that smelled of lavender, followed by all kinds of elaborate maneuvers with a blow dryer and curling iron.

Beside her, Twiggy was getting the same treatment from Ricardo's assistant who piled her hair into an artfully messy topknot, complete with ringlets that framed her face. Holly loved their new hairdos, especially hers. French braids woven with ribbons and tiny silk rosebuds was a whole lot more glamorous than a plain old pony tail tied back with a scrunchie.

"Wow," Twiggy said. "You look like a princess."

"So do you."

"Duh-uh," Twiggy said. "Let's get a manicure. My nails are the pits." She held up her hands and scowled. "I knew mucking out stalls was a bad idea."

* * *

Sitting on a muck bucket outside Buccaneer's stall, Kate cleaned tack while she waited for Will. It was already past four, and he'd told her three o'clock for their lesson.

"Don't worry," Jude said. "He'll show up."

As if on cue, a bright red convertible drove into the yard. Wearing a shirt that matched his car, Will unfolded his lanky frame from the driver's seat. He glanced at the darkening sky, then raised the top.

"Use the indoor to warm up," he told Kate. "If it doesn't rain, we'll work outside."

Leo sauntered by, hands in his pockets. He gave Kate a friendly nod and kept going—no sign of Margot and her groupies. The yard was quiet; even the grooms were taking a much-needed break before evening feed. Jennifer and Bridget had gone to the village. They'd offered to buy Polo mints for Buccaneer.

As Kate saddled her horse, she wondered what Holly and Twiggy were doing. Probably squealing over clothes and giving each other makeovers. Was it about to rain in London? Would their party shoes get wet as they raced to the Dorchester? Kate had Googled the event and found out where it was, then hated herself for doing it.

She didn't care. She really didn't—lessons with Nicole and Will were far more important than hanging out with a bunch of ultra-rich directors and spoiled movie stars who didn't know one end of a horse from the other.

The rain held off, so after Kate and Buccaneer warmed up, Will had them transfer to the outdoor school where he'd set up a line of gymnastics—cross-rails with poles on top, about two-and-a-half feet high. After one pass, Will called her into the center of the arena.

"Ride your horse from back to front," he said. "Don't

steer the front end. The engine's in the back—that's where all the power and energy come from, and it's your job to tell that energy where to go."

"Okay." Kate nodded. "Got it."

"Your legs are the gas pedal." He patted her boot. "They create impulsion, the rpms of your engine."

Clearly, Will Hunter was a car nut. Had he trained his red convertible to do half passes and flying changes? Kate gave a little cough to hide her smile.

"And when you jump a line," Will went on, "concentrate on a focal point—something fixed, like a fence post or a tree. It will help you stay centered."

Kate took the jumps again.

She focused straight ahead, then realized it was Leo—not a fence post—in her line of sight. He smiled and gave her a thumbs-up as she cleared the last jump. Feeling oddly pleased, Kate cantered toward Will.

"Better," he said. "But soften your hands a bit more."

Giving Buccaneer a little more rein, Kate jumped the brush, a hogsback, and two double oxers. She did a rollback and jumped them from the other direction. Then Will had her switch to flat work, trotting in circles and bending around traffic cones. Leo was still there, watching.

Kate patted Buccaneer's sweaty neck.

"That's enough for today," Will said. "He's coming along nicely, so let's not push him too hard."

Would he offer another private lesson? Just then, his cell phone rang and he turned away. Gathering up her reins, Kate headed for the gate. Leo stood to one side.

"Nice job," he said.

"Thanks."

"He's a great horse, and I'm glad you rescued him," Leo said, as they walked toward the stables.

"I didn't," Kate said. "Caroline did."

"That's not what I heard."

"Who from?"

"Twiggy," he said. "I was at the show, remember? I saw what happened." Leo opened Buccaneer's stall door, and Kate led him inside. "I'd like to strangle that guy who rode him."

Maybe Leo Zeller wasn't as bad as Kate thought. But his last name kept ringing a bell. She'd heard it before. Okay, so where? On the European grand prix circuit? In *Chronicle of the Horse*? "Does your family ride?" Kate said.

"Just me," Leo said. "My brother's a mountaineer, and my father races powerboats."

Kate wanted to ask about his mother, but decided not to. Maybe he didn't have one, or—

"Mama thinks we're all mad," he said.

"Why?"

"Because we're always charging about, getting hurt and making noise. Well, my father does. His boats will blow your eardrums out."

"What does your mother do?" Kate took off Buccaneer's saddle and threw a cooler on his back. He nuzzled her pockets for a treat.

Leo smiled. "She paints butterflies and moths."

All of a sudden, the penny dropped. "Yanni Zeller?"

"Yes, how did you know?"

"My father's got one of her watercolors in his office," Kate said feeding Buccaneer her last mint. "He's a lepidopterist."

"What's his name?" Leo said.

"Ben McGregor."

"*Professor* Ben McGregor?"

"Yes."

"Wow." Leo gave a low whistle. "My mother has all of his books. According to her, your father walks on water."

Kate grinned. "Really?"

"Yes, really," Leo said. His eyes were the most amazing shade of blue—like a tropical lagoon in a travel brochure—and when he smiled, they crinkled at the corners.

After that, it was easy to talk to him, and Kate found it hard to remember why she'd disliked him in the first place. Leo helped clean Buccaneer's stall and put away his tack. Then they headed to the common room for dinner, still talking a mile a minute—just like old friends. But what made it even better was the horrified look on Margot's face when Leo bypassed her table and took a small one in the corner with Kate.

* * *

Holly gasped when she saw Twiggy's walk-in closet. Wooden hangers, all pointing in the same direction, held a rainbow of outfits with color-coordinated shoes on racks beneath them. Piles of neatly folded sweaters sat on shelves above; wicker baskets contained gloves, scarves, and woolly hats.

"Cripes," Holly said, turning around slowly. "Do you actually wear all this stuff?"

"Not if I can help it," Twiggy said. "My mother's stuck in a time warp. She thinks I'm still eight years old."

One dress was rose pink taffeta with puffed sleeves and a lace collar; another had farm animals scattered all over it. There was even a frilly pinafore that looked like something Little Miss Muffet would wear. Shoving them roughly to one side, Twiggy reached further into the racks and pulled out an armload of evening gowns.

"That's more like it," Holly said.

Twiggy dumped them onto her four-poster bed. "Yeah, and if this lot doesn't work, there's plenty more."

Holly tried one after another. She twirled in front of Twiggy's full-length mirror and shoved her feet into gold sandals with three-inch heels. After changing her mind a dozen times, she chose a sapphire blue cocktail dress with a beaded top and matching purse. This was more fun than Blaines, the boutique in Winfield where she and Kate had bought their dresses for the premiere in New York.

Kate.

A pang of guilt shot through her. But that was crazy. Kate would loathe all this fuss. She'd moan and groan; she'd complain about having to wear makeup, and—

No. It was better that Kate hadn't come. Besides, she'd made it quite clear that she never wanted to see Nathan Crane again. Holly wasn't too keen on seeing him either, but she wanted to hang out with Adam. He'd texted her from

Nathan's phone because his didn't work. They were to meet him at the Dorchester Hotel on Park Lane. Twiggy said it was just around the corner.

A five-minute walk.

But first, they had to bamboozle Twiggy's parents. There'd been no sign of them when they got back from the salon. Twiggy had yelled, "We're home," as they ran up the marble staircase, but nobody answered.

Their footsteps echoed, and Holly gave a little shiver. This wasn't a home; it was more like a museum filled with spindly furniture, oriental rugs you didn't dare walk on, and crystal chandeliers even bigger than the ones at the Royal Mews.

Just then, Twiggy emerged from her closet, pulling on a pair of elbow-length yellow gloves. She handed Holly her cell phone. "I don't have a bag, so stuff it in yours." Then she frowned. "That dress needs something else."

"Like what?"

"This," Twiggy said, and plucked a dazzling gold necklace from a padded jewelry box. She fastened it around Holly's neck. In the center was a cluster of diamonds.

"No, I can't. I might lose it, and—"

Twiggy laughed. "Don't worry, it's fake. The real one is locked up in my father's safe."

"What about you?"

"He'd like to keep me locked up, too."

"No, silly. I mean bling. Aren't you going to wear a bracelet or—?"

"A tiara?" Twiggy said. "You won't catch me in one of those."

"But you're a princess," Holly said.

"Not tonight, remember?"

Holly wasn't too sure about that. In her primrose-yellow ball gown and matching gloves, Twiggy looked exactly like Belle when she danced with the Beast.

* * *

Wearing long raincoats over their party dresses, they escaped without a hitch. Holly never even met Twiggy's parents—they'd left for the opera while the girls were upstairs—and Steffan was now in his room glued to the TV. The sound of gunfire erupted. Twiggy scribbled him a note and tacked it to the door.

Gone to Claudia's. Home tomorrow.

"What if he follows us?" Holly said. She had visions of Steffan appearing at the hotel and dragging them off by their ears like naughty children.

"He won't," Twiggy said as they walked past the American Embassy in Grosvenor Square. "He's watching a James Bond special."

A stream of limos and luxury cars pulled up at the Dorchester and disgorged one glittering celebrity after another, including Giles Ballantine with Nathan's glamorous co-star clinging to his arm. Dressed in clouds of white chiffon, Tess O'Donnell gave the photographers a dazzling smile before disappearing inside.

Holly took a deep breath and followed.

She was so focused on dodging the crowd that she hardly

noticed the hotel's famous topiary horse amid a bed of yellow pansies in the front garden.

Glass doors swished open. Holly breezed through them and had barely taken two steps into the foyer when Adam shot out from behind a marble column and pulled her into a bone-crunching hug. Then he kissed her.

Twiggy gasped. "Nathan?"

"No, I'm Adam," he said, bowing. "And you must be—"

"B-b-belle," Twiggy stammered. Wide-eyed, she looked from Adam to Holly and back again. "I thought, I mean—like wow, you look *just* like him."

Even though she'd warned Twiggy about this, Holly wasn't surprised she'd muddled them up. In school, Adam and Nathan had often swapped clothes to confuse their teachers, and at the premiere in New York Adam boasted that he'd signed more autographs than Nathan had.

Adam flicked an imaginary speck of lint off the lapels of his tuxedo. "But I'm better looking."

"Show-off," Holly said and punched him.

He staggered backward, hand on his chest. "Ouch! Now I know you're *really* here."

Holly punched him again—gently this time.

17

A SMALL ORCHESTRA WAS PLAYING show tunes when they reached the Dorchester's grand ballroom. Waiters circled with trays of champagne; well-dressed people drifted from one buffet table to another. Surrounded by admirers, Nathan stood with his arm draped casually around Tess O'Donnell. Blond ringlets escaped from the mass of curls piled on top of her head.

"She looks just like you," Holly whispered to Twiggy.

"Me?" Adam said.

Holly took a step toward him, but Adam dodged sideways and took Twiggy's arm. "Come on," he said. "Let's get something to eat before she decks me again."

After they vanished into the crowd, someone else claimed Tess O'Donnell's attention, and Nathan was momentarily alone. Glass in hand, he turned around, and his face lit up when he saw Holly. He hurried toward her.

She hadn't expected that.

The last time she'd seen Nathan was at the premiere when Kate had caused a firestorm on his Facebook page by dumping him in front of Giles Ballantine and all his astonished guests. Then she and Holly had stormed off, leaving Adam to cope with the fallout.

Nathan looked the same—maybe a little bit older, but that was probably because he hadn't shaved. The same lock of streaky blond hair fell across his forehead, the way Adam's always did. His eyes were just as green as Holly remembered.

"Hi," he said. "I'm glad you came."

"Yeah, me, too."

Then he surprised her even more. "Tell Kate I'm sorry, okay? I never meant to hurt her."

Holly opened her mouth and shut it again. She was still trying to process this when Adam and Twiggy raced up, plates brimming with yummy looking appetizers.

"Well, hello," Nathan said. "Who are you?"

"She's a princess," Adam blurted.

Holly nudged him so hard, a shrimp fell off his plate. "Idiot," she said. "I told you not to—"

"It's okay," Twiggy said.

With a shy smile, she held out her hand. But instead of shaking it, Nathan shocked Holly for a third time by raising Twiggy's hand to his lips and kissing it. Then, without missing a beat, he whisked her onto the dance floor.

The orchestra was playing the theme from *Beauty and the Beast*.

* * *

Adam pointed out one celebrity after another—a rock star Holly had never heard of, two British film producers, and an elderly duchess with a face like boiled leather. She carried a fluffy white dog in her purse. It bared its yellow teeth at anyone who stepped near, including a harried looking guy from the U.S. embassy who spent ten minutes apologizing to the duchess for upsetting her dog.

"He's an attaché," Adam said.

"Okay," Holly said. "I'll bite. What does an attaché do?"

"He attaches stuff to other stuff."

Holly giggled. "Idiot."

She was about to finish off Twiggy's abandoned cheese puffs when Giles Ballantine ambled over with Tess O'Donnell. She'd been super grateful for the riding lessons Holly and Kate had given her last summer, but at the *Moonlight* premiere in April, she'd ignored both of them.

"Great to see you again," she gushed, as if she'd suddenly remembered who Holly was. Giles Ballantine had probably clued her in.

"Where's young Kate?" he said, stroking his beard. It was bushier than ever. "I thought she was coming."

"She's—" Adam began.

Holly cut him off. "Kate's in Cornwall, taking care of your old horse."

"Pirate," Giles Ballantine said, "right?"

"Try again." Holly knew she was being rude but couldn't

stop herself. How could anyone forget a horse like Buccaneer?

He shrugged. "Sorry, I can't remember."

"Does it matter?" Tess said. "It's just a dumb animal."

Holly gritted her teeth so hard she was surprised they didn't crack. In Giles Ballantine's privileged world, horses were status symbols, like Ferraris and mansions in Beverly Hills. Until a few months ago, Holly had entertained visions of a career in film—set design or costumes—but now she wasn't so sure. Movie moguls like Giles Ballantine lived on another planet. So did Tess O'Donnell and Nathan Crane.

Just then he ran up, holding hands with Twiggy. Her face was flushed; her eyes sparkled. She couldn't seem to stop smiling. Holly figured she'd talk about this forever.

"Hey, GB," Nathan said. "This is Belle."

The movie director regarded Twiggy as if she were a prize cow. Holly half expected him to walk around her to see what she looked like from the back. Finally, he said, "You'd make a good stand-in for my star." He patted Tess's arm, still draped over his. "What do you think?"

Tess yawned. "Yeah, sure."

"What does a stand-in do?" Twiggy said.

Adam grinned. "Stand around?"

"It's a boring job," Nathan said. "You're either freezing cold or stuck under arc lamps for hours, getting hot and sweaty, while the director, the cameraman, and the gaffer argue about angles and lighting."

"Gaffer?" Twiggy said.

"The lighting engineer."

"Okay, so what are the actors doing while the stand-ins are"—Twiggy glanced at Nathan—"standing around?"

"Goofing off in their dressing rooms."

"Not me," Tess said. "I'm rehearsing my lines." She tugged at Giles Ballantine's arm. "Can we go now?"

The director pulled an elaborate gold pocket watch from inside his dinner jacket and flicked it open. "Not yet," he said. "You and Nathan must leave together. There are fans waiting outside. Let's not disappoint them, okay?"

"But I'm exhausted," Tess whined. "Can't someone else do it?"

"I will," Twiggy said.

Nathan thumped Adam on the back. "And you can go with her because I'm exhausted, too."

* * *

To Holly's surprise, Giles Ballantine didn't argue. He moved them into a private room and barked orders like a drill sergeant.

"Girls, you must swap dresses, and Tess will keep out of sight. The rest of you"—he fixed his steely gray eyes upon Holly—"don't talk about this." Then he summoned an assistant and told him to order the limo. "Ten minutes, out front."

Holly peeked around the door. The party was winding down. Some of the guests had already left, and waiters had begun to clear tables, but the orchestra was still playing. She hadn't even danced with Adam yet.

"Come on," she said.

"We can dance when I get back."

"Now," Holly said. "Let's go."

As they bounced about, Holly remembered the first time they'd danced together at a Timber Ridge party when Holly was still in her wheelchair. Adam had grabbed the handles and swung her around till she got dizzy, like he was doing now. He was almost seventeen; in another year he'd be off to college. Holly didn't even want to think about it. The music stopped.

"Here comes my partner-in-crime," Adam said as Twiggy floated toward them in Tess's white dress. Its chiffon scarves hung in a tangle down her back. While Holly sorted them out, Nathan whipped off Adam's bow tie and loosened his collar, then mussed up his hair. Adam hadn't shaved that morning, either.

Doppelgängers, Holly thought.

It was freaky how much Adam and Twiggy looked like Nathan and Tess. You'd never know it wasn't them unless you stood really close or had a powerful camera like those pushy paparazzi. Hopefully they'd gotten enough pictures earlier and had gone off to annoy other celebrities. London was full of them.

Someone announced that the limo had arrived. Adam slipped into place beside Twiggy. "Wish us luck," he said to Holly.

She snapped off a bunch of photos. They looked so cute together that she felt a pang of jealousy. Adam winked at her. He loved being in the limelight.

"Come on," he said, cupping Twiggy's elbow. "Our fans await us." As they left the room, Giles Ballantine hustled after them. So did Holly, but Nathan pulled her back.

"Stay with me."

"But I want to watch," Holly said.

"No problem," Nathan said. "We'll have front-row seats." He took her hand and led her into another room with a huge window that overlooked Dorchester's grand entrance. "See?"

Down below, a restless crowd strained against the police barrier; a long black limo crouched at the curb like a panther waiting to pounce. From beneath the hotel's awning, the golden couple emerged. Twiggy waved; Adam blew kisses. They held hands and hammed it up for the cameras.

Twiggy had to be *loving* this.

Fans cheered and held up cell phones, taking pictures like mad. No sign of any paparazzi or TV cameras. The limo's tinted front window rolled down part way, and Holly caught sight of a bearded face. That was odd. Chauffeurs didn't normally have beards, did they? Maybe it was Giles Ballantine at the wheel. She looked again, but the window had closed.

After giving the fans another round of extravagant air kisses, Adam helped Twiggy into the limo's back seat. One of her scarves got caught in the door and it took a few moments to extricate it. Then, as the car glided off, Adam and Twiggy waved out the open window like a pair of real movie stars. Holly felt tears spring to her eyes.

"What happens now?" she said.

"They'll cruise down Park Lane, then drive around back and into the underground garage," Nathan said. "Adam and Belle will come in through the hotel's kitchen door as the trash is being taken out." He grinned. "Glamorous, huh?"

"How long will it take?" Holly said.

"About five minutes." Nathan looked thoughtful for a moment, then said, "I like Belle, so why don't you tell me who she really is?"

Holly hesitated. Twiggy had wanted to be incognito tonight, but given how things turned out, she probably wouldn't mind if Nathan knew the truth. So Holly filled him in. But when she got to the part about Twiggy's father insisting on a bodyguard whenever his daughter was in London, she couldn't get the image of that bearded chauffeur out of her mind.

It had to have been Giles Ballantine.

But it wasn't. He was already back in the ballroom chatting with a few remaining guests when Nathan and Holly returned. Her anxiety level rose another notch.

"What's wrong?" Nathan said.

She told him, even though she had nothing to go on except a vague suspicion that something wasn't right. "I'm worried."

"Don't be," he said. "GB's assistant ordered the limo. It's from the studio's most reliable rental service, and I've used it a dozen times."

"Did any of the drivers have a beard?"

"I don't know, probably," Nathan said. "They come and go pretty fast, but they've all been thoroughly vetted."

Holly managed a weak smile. "Like a horse."

The lights dimmed and the orchestra struck up a slow number. "Sounds like the last dance," Nathan said.

He gave a little bow and reminded Holly of the dashing hero he'd played in *Moonlight*. She slid into his arms and promptly added another layer of worry to the ones she already had.

Was dancing with Nathan Crane being disloyal to Kate?

* * *

Ten minutes went by, then thirty. Holly couldn't stop looking at her watch. "Shouldn't they be back by now?"

"Traffic," Nathan said. "It's Saturday night. The streets are probably jammed, so stop worrying. Giles isn't."

"Of course he isn't," Holly snapped. "It's not his stars who've gone missing; it's my boyfriend and a princess."

"They are *not* missing," Nathan said. "They're out there having a great time. I bet the driver has taken them on a sightseeing tour."

"In heavy traffic?" Holly checked her watch again. "At midnight?"

"So call them," Nathan said. "Oh, wait a minute. Adam's phone doesn't work over here."

"But Twiggy's does," Holly said. She opened her purse and groaned. "Oh, no."

"What's wrong now?"

Holly held up Twiggy's iPhone. "She left it with me."

"Then I guess we'll just have to wait." With a yawn, Nathan pointed toward an ornate silver urn surrounded by a forest of dainty cups and saucers. "Coffee?"

"Might as well," Holly said. "I won't sleep anyway."

"Where are you guys staying?" Nathan poured two cups of coffee and gave one to Holly. She sank into an overstuffed armchair.

"At Claudia's house. She's Twiggy's cousin, but I don't know where she lives."

Twiggy hadn't even given Holly the phone number. But why would she? They didn't know that Twiggy was going to—

Holly's hand shook and coffee splattered down the front of Twiggy's gorgeous blue dress. She *had* to stop worrying. Twiggy was having the time of her life, swanning all over London with Adam and pretending to be a star. Right now, they were probably signing autographs in Piccadilly Circus.

The head waiter approached Nathan. "I'm sorry, sir, but we have to close up."

"No problem," Nathan said. "But can you have fresh coffee sent up to my suite?"

"Certainly, sir."

"Come along." Nathan hauled Holly to her feet. "We'll hang out upstairs. Giles booked half the top floor, so you can have your own room."

Did he expect her to sleep at the hotel? Then again, she didn't have much choice. No way could she go back to Twiggy's by herself. Twiggy's father, Lord DuBois or Prince whatever he was called, would kill her for misplacing his daughter.

18

NATHAN'S SUITE WAS LIKE A HOLLYWOOD set from the 1930s—brocade draperies, plaster cherubs on the ceiling, and carpets thick enough to get lost in. Beyond a balcony that overlooked Hyde Park, trees sparkled with a bazillion fairy lights. Even the topiary horse was all lit up.

Holly was too frantic to notice.

She checked her watch again. Twiggy and Adam had been gone for well over an hour. Room service delivered a pot of fresh coffee and almond scones, still warm from the oven.

"Hungry?" Nathan said.

Holly's stomach rumbled. All she'd eaten since lunch were Twiggy's leftover cheese puffs. "Yes . . . um, no. I don't know."

"Well, that narrows it down," Nathan said, grinning.

"I want you to call the cops."

"And tell them what, exactly?" Nathan bit into a scone. "A stretch limo driven by a bearded man has just absconded with my best friend and a princess?"

"That'll do for a start."

Feeling utterly helpless, Holly pressed her nose against the window and stared at her distorted reflection. There had to be *something* she could do, but Nathan was right. All they had were suspicions, and they were as flimsy as butterfly wings. The police would dismiss them, politely of course, then they'd carry on chasing real criminals. A siren blared down Park Lane.

It jolted Holly's brain into action.

There *was* something they could do. She rounded on Nathan. "Call the limo service. Ask if their driver had a beard."

"I don't have the number."

"Then get it from Giles's assistant," Holly snapped.

In quick succession, Nathan made two calls. He shook his head. "The driver was a woman."

"It wasn't," Holly said. "I saw a guy with a beard."

"And a patch over one eye?"

Close to tears, Holly flung herself onto Nathan's couch. She grabbed a velvet pillow and hung onto it like a life raft. Nobody but her cared about Adam and Twiggy. Nathan clearly thought she was making a fuss over nothing. The door banged open and Giles Ballantine strode into the room.

"Are they back?" he said.

"Not yet."

"That's *my* nickel they're driving around on," said the movie director. "This gallivanting about is costing me money. Find out where they are, and tell that driver to get them back here, pronto."

"Yes, sir."

Holly heaved a sigh of relief. Finally, somebody else was worried, even if it was only over his stupid bank account and not two of Holly's best friends. If anything happened to them, she'd—

Nathan's cell phone rang. He listened, turned a little pale, then handed it to Giles Ballantine.

"What's wrong?" Holly said.

He held up a warning finger. "Wait."

For what felt like ten minutes but was probably ten seconds, Holly watched Giles Ballantine turn pale as well. He nodded a few times, then hung up and cleared his throat. "It seems we have a—a situation."

"Like what?" Holly wanted to shake it out of him, but for once the director seemed at a loss for words.

Nathan took over. "The rental service put a tracer on their limo."

"And?"

"It's been abandoned," he said, looking directly at Holly. "And you were right about the driver. He was a last-minute replacement."

Holly's blood ran cold. "Adam and Twiggy?"

"They've disappeared."

"Like . . . they've been *kidnapped*?"

But that was ridiculous. It made absolutely no sense. Who in their right minds would hold Adam and Twiggy for ransom, unless—?

A wall of guilt slammed into Holly so hard, she almost choked. "Twiggy's bodyguard. We should've—"

"It's not your fault," Nathan said.

Tearfully, she said, "Yes, it is."

"I don't think they were after the princess."

"What do you mean?"

"Whoever they were," Nathan said, "it's Tess and me they wanted."

Holly sucked in her breath. Had the bad guys tried to snatch Nathan before? She knew he had a bodyguard, but she'd never really questioned why. Was he here tonight—one of the well-dressed guests with a gun hidden beneath his tuxedo? Holly fumbled for her phone. Twiggy had told her to dial 999 if she ever needed emergency help in England—and if this didn't qualify as a full-blown emergency, she didn't know what did.

"I'm calling the police."

"Let's not go *that* far," Giles Ballantine said. "I'm sure there's a reasonable explanation."

"There isn't," Holly cried. "They've been kidnapped, you idiot. *Do* something. Don't just stand here like a—" Desperately, she looked at Nathan. Where was his explosive temper when you needed it?

"Take it easy," he said.

Shoving Nathan to one side, Holly pounded the director

with both fists. Startled, he took a step back and straightened his tuxedo.

"Giles, why don't you call the embassy?" Nathan said, pulling Holly away from him. "They'll know what to do."

"Yes," Holly yelled. "Call somebody, anybody who can—" She choked up again.

This wasn't happening.

It was a nightmare and she'd wake up in a minute at Cousin Claudia's house and they'd all have a good laugh about it—never mind that she didn't have a clue what Claudia looked like or where she lived.

* * *

The attaché Adam had pointed out earlier arrived in less than ten minutes. With him was a tall, brown-haired man who showed them his badge. "Detective Inspector Morgan," he said.

Prompted by Nathan, Giles Ballantine explained the situation. He made it sound like the plot of a horrible movie. "Mistaken identity."

"Then we'll have to tread even more carefully," said the inspector.

"Why?" Holly said.

"The kidnappers obviously think they've got Mr. Crane and Miss O'Donnell," Inspector Morgan said. "And it's best if they go on thinking that"—he paused—"because if they realize their mistake, then . . ." His words trailed off.

After that, there were lots of phone calls, and then more

police showed up. With grave faces, they took statements from Holly and Nathan. Giles Ballantine sent for Tess. She arrived looking rumpled and sleepy and not at all happy when the inspector said she'd have to go into hiding. So would Nathan. If either of them showed their famous faces in public, the kidnappers would—

"What?" Holly said.

"Let's not go there, miss," said the inspector sounding quite fatherly, "unless we have to."

But suppose Adam or Twiggy convinced the kidnappers they weren't two famous movie stars but just a couple of ordinary kids—well, except for Twiggy being a princess. What then?

Holly's head spun, her legs trembled. Vaguely she heard the inspector telling them to keep this under wraps. No press, no interviews. Nobody else must know about the kidnapping except for Adam's and Twiggy's parents. Holly couldn't begin to imagine how scared and angry they would be, especially Twiggy's father. He'd go ballistic.

The phone rang; everyone froze.

The ransom?

But it was room service wondering if they wanted any more coffee.

*   *   *

The police installed a wiretap on Giles Ballantine's cell phone and told him how to handle the call when it came. They would be listening in and trying to trace the kidnappers.

"Keep them on the line as long as you can," said Detective Inspector Morgan.

The attaché offered to get in touch with Adam's parents; Giles Ballantine would handle Twiggy's father.

"Will I have to see him?" Holly said, feeling guilty all over again, even though it was Twiggy's decision to bypass Steffan and deceive her parents.

"No," said the inspector. "You can go home."

Holly heaved a sigh of relief. She didn't want to stay in London—it wouldn't do any good. The kidnappers were probably a hundred miles away by now. The best thing she could do for Adam and Twiggy—and for herself—would be to get back to Beaumont Park, patch things up with Kate, and take care of Twiggy's horse.

"I'll order a car," Giles Ballantine said.

"Best not, sir," warned the inspector. "Your car hire service is under investigation. We'll have a policewoman drive Miss Chapman back to Cornwall."

He gave Holly his business card. "If you think of anything else that might be useful, no matter how trivial, ring me right away—day or night."

"Thank you," she said and handed over Twiggy's cell phone. No point in keeping it now. It was dead anyway.

* * *

Dawn was breaking by the time Holly finally fell asleep. She woke at noon and found a note from Nathan on her bedside table.

*We left early, and I didn't want to wake you. I'll text
you from whatever remote dungeon Giles hides us in.
Tess is NOT happy. xxx N*

He sounded almost cheerful, like this was a big adventure
or a movie he was in. What about Adam and Twiggy? Had
anyone heard from the kidnappers?

Holly didn't even know who to ask.

Was Giles Ballantine still at the hotel, or had he hidden
himself as well? Then she spotted the inspector's business
card where she'd dropped it before collapsing into bed. He'd
said to call any time.

He answered on the first ring. "Morgan, here."

"This is Holly Chapman," she said. "Is there any news
about—?" It was a struggle to keep her voice normal.

"No, not yet," he said. "I will let you know the minute
we hear. Now, Constable Yates will drive you home. Can you
be ready to leave in half an hour?"

"Yes," Holly said.

She had nothing to pack—not even a toothbrush. Luckily
the hotel provided one, along with fluffy towels and plenty of
hot water.

After a quick shower, she climbed into Twiggy's blue
dress and stuffed her yellow ball gown into a brown paper
bag. It would get all crumpled but Twiggy wouldn't care.

Twiggy!

She had to be scared stiff. Adam, too. Desperately, Holly
looked for someone to blame for all this, but kept coming
back to herself. If she'd just stayed in Cornwall, none of this

would've happened; Adam and Twiggy would be safe. Feeling miserable, she took the elevator downstairs.

Constable Yates met her in the foyer. Holly had been expecting one of those traditional English Bobbies with the funny looking helmets, but this woman wore a cute navy hat and a checked scarf tucked neatly into a crisp white shirt.

She showed Holly her badge. "You ready to leave?"

"Yes," Holly said. She'd never been so ready to leave a place in her life.

* * *

As they headed west out of London, Constable Yates pointed out places of interest along the way, but Holly was in too much of a funk to pay attention. She apologized, and the travelogue ceased. On went the radio. Holly closed her eyes and dozed off. Next thing she knew they were slowing down.

Holly yawned. "Something wrong?"

"Traffic jam," said Constable Yates. "We'll take a detour."

"Where are we?"

All Holly could see were farms and fields with high hedgerows and metal gates with cows poking their heads over.

"Just south of Exeter, in Devon," the constable said, turning right off the main road. A signpost ahead pointed toward 'Dartmoor National Park.'

Holly sat up in a hurry. "Are we going through *Dartmoor*?"

"It'll be faster than being stuck in traffic all the way to Plymouth." The constable turned on her GPS. "We might even see some ponies." She glanced at Holly. "Do you like horses?"

"You bet," Holly said and told Constable Yates all about Timber Ridge and the riding team and why she was at Beaumont Park. "My best friend is there, too."

But was Kate still her best friend?

In a couple of hours, she would find out. But for now, she was going to take her mind off Twiggy and Adam by taking a bazillion pictures of ponies. Maybe she'd get one of that adorable chestnut that Kate said looked just like Tapestry.

19

KATE HAD JUST FINISHED GROOMING Buccaneer and was sitting on a bench texting with Brad when a nondescript black car drove into the yard. It parked too far away for Kate to see who it was—probably a potential student or somebody come to check out a horse. They showed up almost every day.

Her phone pinged.

More bad news from Brad. He was helping the riding team at the Hampshire Classic. Things weren't going well. Kristina James got eliminated in cross-country, both Sue and Robin scored low on their dressage tests, and Angela had just racked up sixteen faults in show jumping.

Timber Ridge was in second-to-last place.

Mrs. Dean was on the warpath and threatening to fire Liz. She'd done this before, and Liz always insisted it was an empty threat. But Kate worried anyway. If Liz lost her job, she'd lose the house as well. Kate was about to text Brad again when she heard wheels crunching on gravel. The car had pulled a little closer, and this time she saw the driver quite clearly. Her uniform looked familiar.

A policewoman?

The passenger door opened, and Holly stepped out wearing a long blue dress that glittered in the late afternoon sun. Kate stared at the car, then at Holly, who was clutching a brown paper bag like a lifeline. Yesterday, she'd left town in a golden coach, and now she'd just returned in a pumpkin. So, where was Twiggy? And why a police car? Had they been arrested?

Kate leaped to her feet.

Brad and the riding team would have to wait. She stuffed the phone in her pocket and sprinted toward Holly. Those idiotic gold sandals weren't made for walking in . . .

Holly stumbled. In a flash Kate caught her before she landed in a heap. "Are you okay?"

"Yeah," Holly said as her police escort drove off. "And I'm sorry."

"Me, too."

Holly limped along beside her. "My fault."

"No, it's mine." Kate helped Holly into the tack room and closed the door. She took a deep breath. This wasn't going to be easy, but she had to plunge in fast before she wimped out. "Look, I know you were protecting my feelings, about Nathan's party and stuff. And it's okay. I understand."

"Seriously?"

"Yes," Kate said. "Seriously."

Hitching up her skirt, Holly sank into a metal chair. "I'm never quite sure what you're feeling."

"Neither am I," Kate said.

It felt good to say that, to get it out in the open. She was tired of bottling stuff up. Holly didn't. She always said what she wanted to say, and you always knew where you stood with her. Well, maybe not always, like right now.

"What's up with the police?" Kate went on. "Did you and Twiggy get in trouble?"

To her surprise, Holly burst into tears. Kate glanced at the clock. Fifteen minutes till evening feed. She'd better get Holly upstairs and hope they didn't run into Margot and her minions along the way.

* * *

For once, the yard was quiet, and nobody saw them slip into the house. Their room, thank goodness, was empty. Kate shut the door and leaned against it. Holly sat on Kate's bunk. Between sobs and gulps of air, she blurted out what happened in London.

Kate felt herself turn pale. *"Kidnapped?"*

"Yes," Holly whispered. "But don't tell anyone, promise? I shouldn't even be telling you. We have to keep it a secret, or—"

She dissolved into tears again. This was almost more of a shock than her horrible news. Holly never cried. Kate pulled her into a clumsy hug, not sure what else to do. Would Holly flip out? Did she need some sort of counseling, like with a shrink? Well, one thing was for sure. They couldn't sit here forever because already Kate could hear voices on the other side of their door. It opened.

Jennifer said, "Hey, you're—"

"Don't tell," Holly whispered.

Kate covered her with a blanket. "Lie down and keep quiet."

"What's up with her?" Jennifer said. "And where's Twig?"

"They, um—" Kate scrambled for answers. "They had a big fight. Twiggy's still in London."

She felt Holly kick her. It was a dumb excuse, but what else could she say? Jennifer was curious. Everyone would be. They all knew that Twiggy had taken Holly home for the weekend and that they had planned on getting their hair done at a fancy salon and having a sleepover with Twiggy's cousin.

"Bummer," Jennifer said. She got busy changing into barn clothes. "I'll take care of Gemini if you want."

"Yeah, thanks," Kate said. "That'd be great."

"No worries."

The moment she left, Holly sat up. Her hair was a tangled mess, her face streaked with tears. She really did look as if she'd just had a big breakup. "Thanks—and I'm sorry I kicked you."

"S'okay."

"Guess I'd better change, huh?" Holly said, tugging at her dress. A handful of blue beads fell off and scattered across the floor. "Can't do barn chores in this."

* * *

Kate managed to keep reality at arm's length until halfway through supper when it thudded into her like a bag of hammers. No wonder Holly had freaked out. She'd struggled through evening feed with a fake smile, then begged off dinner and eaten a sandwich in their room. Grabbing two apples and a handful of cookies, Kate ran upstairs to join her.

Holly said, "I can't stop thinking about them."

"Me neither," Kate said. "But we must."

"Why?" Holly's hand trembled as she bit into an apple. Juice ran down her chin.

Kate tossed a napkin at her. "Because it won't do any good."

"That's heartless."

"It's not," Kate said. "It's common sense."

"That's half your problem, Kate McGregor," Holly said. "You have too much common sense." She caught her breath. "And I don't have nearly enough. I should never have let Twiggy leave Steffan behind. If he'd been there, he'd have—"

"—probably been kidnapped as well," Kate finished. She knew that wasn't true. Twiggy's bodyguard would've pulled a gun on the kidnappers and that would've been that. End of problem. "Look, I'm as scared and worried as you are, and I wish we could tell someone, but we can't."

"So what *can* we do?"

"We pretend everything is fine. Jennifer's the only one who thinks you're upset over a fight with Twiggy. And I'll tell her to keep quiet about it, okay?"

"Okay." Holly wiped her eyes with the napkin. "It's hard."

"I know," Kate said. This was the awful part, sitting about feeling helpless while poor Adam and Twiggy were—

On the bed, Holly's beaded purse gave a muffled squawk. They both froze; then Kate whipped out the phone. No caller ID. She thrust it at Holly.

"Hello?" Holly said.

"The inspector?" Kate whispered.

Holly nodded, but didn't speak.

Kate bit her lip. This was worse than waiting for winners to be announced at a horse show. No, that wasn't even close. This was far, far worse. This was—

Holly hung up. "They've asked for a ransom."

"How much?"

"He didn't say," Holly said. "But Twiggy and Adam are all right. Giles talked to them."

"So, where are they?"

"He's not sure, but he thinks they're out to sea."

"Cripes," Kate said. "The ocean is *enormous*." They'd be impossible to find, like searching for rare butterflies in the Amazon jungle. Her father had tried, and Kate knew how tough it was. "Well, you know what this means, don't you?"

"What?"

"The kidnappers haven't figured out they've got the wrong kids," Kate said. "Otherwise they wouldn't have asked for a ransom." She had no idea if this were true, but if it helped Holly to feel better, she would bend the truth until it snapped.

Holly sighed. She set her phone on Kate's lap and swiped the screen. Up came an image; two seconds later it vanished. "Okay, who was in that picture?"

"Like, duh-uh," Kate said. Who else could it be? Blond couple, rumpled tuxedo, and a white dress swathed in scarves—same as the one she'd worn for her *Moonlight* scene. "It's Nathan and Tess, of course."

"Try again." Holly tapped the icon.

Kate stared at the phone. "Wow! Score one for Twiggy and Adam." She slapped Holly a high five. "No wonder they've got those kidnappers fooled."

* * *

The next morning, Holly was convinced she'd blab about the kidnapping if Kate wasn't there to stop her. So they stuck together like burrs on a blanket, cleaning stalls and getting in each other's way. Kate trod on a rake, then tripped over a pitchfork and skidded into a pile of manure. In exasperation she suggested Holly gag herself with duct tape instead.

"Less painful," Kate said, rubbing her leg.

After breakfast, they groomed their horses in tandem. Kate picked out Spud's feet while Holly brushed him; Holly pulled the tangles from Buccaneer's tail, leaving Kate to cope with all the mud he'd rolled in the night before. They even helped each other tack up.

"What's the matter?" Margot sneered as she walked past on Oberon. "Can't put your own saddle on any more?"

"I forgot how," Holly said. "Silly me."

Kate hid her anxiety beneath Spud's saddle flap and

tightened his girth. So far, so good. Holly had managed to keep a lid on it, which wasn't easy for her. At home, she'd always talk first and think later, never mind the fallout.

"Heads up," Will yelled. "Let's go."

Riding Gemini, he led them to the covered school. After warming up their horses and getting the kinks out, they headed for the cross-country course. Kate rode next to Holly; ahead of them, Leo rode beside Jennifer, chattering non-stop the way he had with Kate on Saturday.

Holly scowled. "What's up with him?"

In all the trauma over Adam and Twiggy, Kate had completely forgotten to mention that she'd hung out with Leo after her lesson. Quickly, she whispered a few details. "And his mom paints butterflies."

"Oh, well, in *that* case," Holly said, rolling her eyes, "no problem."

Will gathered his students into a semicircle. "I already know what your horses are capable of, but what I need to know now is what *you* are capable of." He looked at each rider in turn. "So first, we're going to ride the course without jumping to get you familiar with it."

From what Kate had seen already, the fences were traditional—rustic rails, logs, ditches, and banks. No sign of any oddball jumps like picnic tables and umbrellas or a truck bed filled with flowers—or, heaven forbid, a giant wooden mushroom. Kate patted Buccaneer's neck. He'd probably have a meltdown if she asked him to jump a mushroom.

Will said, "We don't go for the crazy stuff here, not for

training anyway." He shot Kate a lopsided grin as if he'd just read her mind. "We save the eye candy for later."

Leo groaned. "But I want to jump a boat."

"That comes next week," Will said. "And an airplane."

The novice course covered two miles of rolling meadows filled with grass even greener than Vermont's, neatly clipped hedgerows, and trails that wound gently through spacious woods that reminded Kate of a park. At one point, as they trotted over the crest of a hill, Smuggler's Island came into view, looking wild and remote with waves pounding its tiny beach.

Holly pointed. "There's the pirate ship."

"Looks like a Bertram to me," Leo said, shading his eyes from the sun. "Fifty footer, at least."

"How can you tell?" Holly snapped. "Boats all look alike."

"So do horses." Leo grinned. "My father's got one."

"A horse?"

"No, a boat."

"Boats are dumb," Holly said. "They—"

"Come on," Kate said. When Holly got like this, she could argue the hind leg off a donkey. "Will's waiting for us."

He stopped at all fifteen jumps to explain their unique features—spreads, awkward angles, drop-offs, spooky-looking ditches—and how best to approach them. After this, they would school their horses over one or two fences each day until they got them right.

"This is stupid," Margot complained. "You've seen one coffin jump, you've seen them all."

"Pity she's not actually *in* it," Jennifer said.

Holly giggled. So did Kate. It felt good to laugh at something instead of worrying all the time. After examining the last jump for every possible pitfall, they followed Will back to the yard. For a few glorious moments, cantering across the fields and sloshing through streams, Kate forgot about Twiggy and Adam and lost herself in Buccaneer's powerful stride.

If only Tapestry were here to share it.

Magician, too. She glanced at Holly, pounding along beside her on Spud, and knew, without a doubt, that she was thinking the exact same thing.

20

SOMEHOW THEY GOT THROUGH Nicole's dressage lesson without a hitch. No major flub-ups, no awkward questions from Margot or the others. Kate began to breathe easier.

Then came the six o'clock news.

She and Holly were in the common room, stuffing themselves with shepherd's pie and hoping there'd be time for dessert before rushing out to help with chores, when they heard an ear-piercing squeal.

"Omigod, it's *him*."

All eyes turned toward the TV. Images flashed like a slideshow on Flickr. The reporter's breathless voice rose to fever pitch, louder and louder, as if one of Hollywood's rising stars was about to win an Oscar.

"No," Holly gasped. "It's—"

"Sshh," Kate said as her fork clattered to the floor.

The room was in an uproar. Margot shrieked. Harriet

pretended to faint—or maybe she really had—and Zoe jumped up and down like the birthday princess at a Disney party. Even Bridget let out a scream as the camera zoomed onto Nathan Crane's famous face. He snarled and shook his fist; someone jerked him away.

But the damage was done.

Thanks to the paparazzi, everyone now knew that Nathan Crane and Tess O'Donnell—mysteriously missing since the big celebration in London—were alive and well at a romantic getaway on the Isle of Skye.

Even worse, the kidnappers knew.

"Let's go," Kate said.

But Holly sat there, looking stunned, as if all the bits hadn't yet fallen into place. "Why?"

"Because your phone's about to ring."

Kate yanked Holly to her feet so fast that her chair fell over. Pushing past a couple of grooms, they stumbled outside. Evening feed was about to begin, so where to go? Their bedroom? No, somebody would interrupt. How about—?

Holly's phone buzzed.

She answered, as if still in a daze, and Kate leaned closer, desperate to hear. *Change of plans*, said the inspector's gravelly voice. Now that the kidnappers knew they'd got the wrong kids, the police had to proceed even more carefully. Adam and Twiggy were at high risk.

Like more than before?

Kate clenched her fists. She wanted to punch the paparazzi who'd done this. No, she wanted to punch *all* of them. Those miserable photographers had no morals; they just trampled over people's lives because all they cared about was making yet another news-grabbing headline.

No wonder Nathan hated them.

* * *

All the air left Holly's body at once. It was like falling off a horse and getting whumped in the gut and not being able to get your breath back. Leaning against Kate, she stuffed the phone in her pocket.

Grooms rushed past, carrying buckets and armloads of hay. Horses banged on stall doors; others whinnied from the fields. Mac issued orders. Holly did her best to help out, but it all seemed so trivial, so terribly unimportant when compared with two scared kids in a boat on the ocean.

Were they tied up?

Holly gulped. She could almost feel the ropes burning into Twiggy's wrists, the wire that bound Adam's ankles. Were they gagged as well? Kate's dumb joke about duct tape sent her spinning sideways. For what seemed like an eternity she stood amid the chaos of evening feed with Kate's arm around her shoulders. Not hugging her exactly, but resting comfortably in case Holly suddenly needed to lean a little harder.

"I've got Gemini," Jennifer said, hefting two buckets at once. "Want me to feed your lot as well?"

"Thanks," Kate said. "But we'll do it."

The others hadn't appeared at evening feed—no surprise

there—except for Leo. He shot them a sympathetic look. Had he somehow guessed what was going on, or was he merely being kind? Holly's feelings about him melted, just a little.

Kate hauled her through the motions.

Dump this in Spud's bucket. Two flakes of hay, not three. Okay, let's give the extra one to Parsley. Watch out for Buccaneer—he wants a Polo.

That, she could handle. Holly fumbled in her pockets and found half a pack covered in lint and bits of hay, but Buccaneer wouldn't care. She dropped three mints into his feed bucket and slipped him another on the side.

"Not too many," Kate warned as Buccaneer slobbered over both of them. "He'll get cavities."

The rest of Holly's evening passed in a blur. Kate tried to keep her distracted with endless card games and a two thousand–piece jigsaw that never seemed any closer to being finished no matter how many people got involved. Kate grumbled that half the pieces were missing. So was the box, which meant that nobody knew what the finished puzzle was supposed to be.

"Wild horses," Leo said. "There's a piece of a mustang's ear in the tack room."

"Eeuw, that's disgusting," Zoe said.

Leo grinned. "And a hoof. I found it in the grain bin."

Holly bit her lip. He reminded her of Adam. That was the sort of idiotic thing he'd say. A tear trickled down her cheek. She wiped it away but not before Margot noticed.

"What's the matter?" she said, oozing fake sympathy. "Has that boyfriend you're always texting with finally dumped you?"

"Nah," Zoe said. "She's allergic to Leo."

Jumping to her feet, Kate pulled Holly up with her. "C'mon, let's go. It stinks in here." Holding her nose, she headed for the door.

Leo sniffed his armpits. "But I just had a shower."

"Did not," Jennifer said. "See that dirt on your knee?"

He looked down. "What's wrong with it?"

"It's the same bit of dirt you had yesterday."

"How do you know?" Leo said, rubbing hard. His knees were tanned and knobby, not nearly as sleek as the rest of him.

"Because—"

They were still squabbling when Holly tore herself away and joined Kate outside. Twilight wrapped them in flickering shadows as they talked in whispers about Magician and Tapestry, about the barn and how much they missed it. Kate admitted to being worried about letting go of Buccaneer for a second time; Holly said she hoped their parents had gone on another date.

Neither of them mentioned Twiggy and Adam. That had become too big to talk about.

A breeze ruffled Holly's hair. She shivered and zipped up her hoodie. It was almost ten. Too early for bed. Besides Holly was dreading sleep. She'd be sure to have nightmares.

* * *

The banging wouldn't stop. Voices screeched, gargoyles jeered, and bony hands gripped her arms like a vise. Mud oozed around her ankles, sucking her down and down—

"Wake up, Holly. Wake up."

"Go away," she moaned.

At least the banging had stopped. But the hands were still there, shaking her like a rag doll. Holly pulled herself free and turned over. She buried her face in a pillow. *Would this nightmare ever end?* Apparently not, because somebody was now yanking off her covers.

"No," Holly wailed and yanked them back.

A gargoyle—or maybe it was Kate—said, "You've gotta get up."

"Why?"

"Because Twiggy's father is here."

The voices, the monsters, the hands all vanished at once. Holly sat up and rubbed her eyes. It was dark, for heaven's sake. "What time is it?"

"Five."

"Say that again."

"Five o'clock, now—"

"No, what you said before. About Twiggy's father." Stiffly, Holly swung herself down from the bunk. Her legs folded the minute she hit the floor. She curled into a ball. Another little nap. That's what she needed.

But Kate hauled her upright, then sat her down firmly on the lower bunk. She dumped Holly's discarded jeans and hoodie on her lap. "Get dressed. You don't want to see Prince Ferdinand in your pajamas."

"I don't want to see him, *period*," Holly said. Then it sunk in. "*Ferdinand?* You've got to be kidding. He's a bull, right?"

"Yes, and so is Twiggy's father," Kate said. "He roared up ten minutes ago in the limo. Made an absolute racket, banging on the front door like a—"

"Bull?" Holly said.

At another time, this would be funny. Like laugh-out-loud funny, because Ferdinand the Bull was a sweet, gentle creature. He liked to sit in the meadow and smell the flowers, not cause a riot by knocking on people's doors before the birds were even up.

He must've been driving all night.

Correction. *Steffan* would've been driving and Prince Ferdinand would've been asleep in the back seat, snoring like a . . . bull. Holly snorted. In the other bunk, Jennifer rolled over but didn't wake up.

"Hustle," Kate said, pulling on her own clothes. "Jude's waiting."

"I want to run away."

Kate sighed. "You can do it after breakfast, and I'll come with you. But first—"

"Yeah, yeah," Holly muttered.

Deep down she'd been expecting this. From what little she knew of Twiggy's father, it was amazing he hadn't come after her sooner, never mind what the police had said about keeping it under wraps. But the goalposts had unexpectedly moved—everyone knew about Tess and Nathan—and now it appeared that Prince Ferdinand the Bull was out for blood.

Hers.

As Holly climbed into her jeans and put her shoes on the wrong feet, she wondered if the inspector knew that Prince Ferdinand was on the rampage.

* * *

Twiggy's father looked nothing like a bull. He was tall and thin with bushy eyebrows and a beaky nose that held his rimless glasses firmly in place. His eyes—hard as marbles—bored into Holly like a dentist's drill. She felt ridiculously small.

Jude said, "This is Holly Chapman. She—"

"Yes, I *know* who she is," said the prince. His voice was even plummier than the queen's. "She's the delinquent who led my daughter astray. If it wasn't for her outrageous behavior, Isabel would be safe at home in her bed."

Delinquent?

Holly bristled. She glanced at Jude, now frowning as if trying to process all this. How much did she know? What idiotic lies had the prince pumped into her already?

He said, leaning toward Jude and jutting his chin, "I want her deported immediately, understand? Send her back to that barbaric place she came from. Get her out of England. She doesn't belong here."

Neither did he, the phony.

Lunaberg didn't exist any more. It was like, what, two hundred years ago when it got swallowed up by Napoleon? He probably choked on it.

"I—um," Jude began. "I'm sure we . . ."

Waving her off, the prince turned on Holly. "If you don't leave right away," he bellowed, prodding her with a bony finger, "I will have you arrested."

Something inside Holly snapped. A white-hot fury flooded her throat and vacuumed up the guilt she'd been drowning in ever since Twiggy disappeared. She felt a nudge against her ankles.

A foot stool? Holly climbed onto it.

"So, *Prince* Ferdinand," she said, now eye-to-eye with him, "you're the father who loves his daughter so much he abandons her in a boarding school and never shows up for sports days and prize givings, right?"

"You don't know what you're—"

"Oh, yes, I do," Holly said. "And I believe you sold Twiggy's old horse that she loved to pieces and bought another one. Did you ask her how she felt about it? No, I didn't think so. You just stuck her with a new horse that's totally wrong for her"—Holly glared at him—"and that scares her to death."

He gaped like a goldfish. "But—"

"And what's more," Holly went on, prodding his chest the way he'd prodded hers, "you hired a trainer who's famous for abusing horses—and riders. But you don't care, do you, Prince Ferdinand? You don't even care enough about Twiggy to say hello when she comes home. You just swan off to the opera. Do you have any idea how hurt she was?"

"She . . . she . . ."

"You're a first-class bully, Prince Ferdinand," Holly said, still prodding. "And it wasn't my idea to sneak out of the house without telling you, it was Twiggy's. She's run away from school, too. Or didn't you know about that either? Maybe your selfish head is buried too deep inside all your precious bank accounts to notice that your kid is unhappy."

"That's ridiculous," he protested. "Isabel's not unhappy. How could she be? She's got everything a girl could possibly want—"

"—except a proper father."

A stunned silence filled the room.

The prince opened his mouth but nothing came out. His eyebrows sagged, his chin drooped. Even his self-satisfied smirk faded. He took a couple of shuffling steps backward.

It wasn't much, but it was enough for Holly. With the sweet taste of victory in her mouth, she stepped off her soapbox and felt Kate's hand on her shoulder.

"Thanks," she whispered.

21

DESPITE HOLLY'S OUTBURST, Jude grounded her. "Stay in your room till I sort things out with the prince."

"There's nothing to sort out," Holly said, eyes blazing. "He's wrong and I'm right, and you'd better warn him to keep quiet about the kidnapping or Inspector Morgan will be slinging *him* in jail, not me."

Twiggy's father made a harrumphing noise, then sniffed and looked down his nose at her. He reminded Kate of an indignant stork—nothing more than bluff and bluster and a few ruffled feathers.

"Let's go," she said. "We're done here."

"Yes," Jude said, sounding grateful. "Take Holly upstairs, and—"

Kate nodded. She knew exactly what Jude wanted: to keep Holly under house arrest.

Fat chance of that.

It'd be easier to stuff lightning in a bottle.

"Why was Jude such a wimp?" Holly said, throwing herself onto Kate's bunk. "She *saw* what Vincent King was like. She *knows* how scared Twiggy is. Why didn't she back me up?"

"Because clients . . . with pots of money."

"Well, I hate it. Mom's not like that."

Kate bit her lip. This was not the time to remind Holly that Liz had danced to Mrs. Dean's tune more than once. She had no choice. Angela's mother ruled Timber Ridge with an iron fist, and if Liz wanted to hold onto her job and the house that came with it, she had to make nice when there was no other way out.

"Now what?" Holly said.

Kate shot a look at Jennifer's empty bed. She'd obviously gotten a head start on morning chores. From next door came the muffled grumbles of others getting up. In twenty minutes, the bathroom would be free. Kate couldn't wait to brush her teeth.

"Breakfast?" she said.

Holly scowled. "Not hungry."

"Don't be an idiot. I'll go down and get something. Crumpets and tea, okay?"

"What*ever*."

"And don't run off," Kate said. "You'd better be here when I get back, or I'll—"

Holly stuck out her tongue, then climbed into the top bunk. "Get me some OJ."

"Please."

Holly rolled her eyes. *"Please."*

"Bratface," Kate said.

If nothing else, that made Holly smile. Kate raced downstairs and into the common room. Leo was hunched over the puzzle. Idly, he flicked the pieces with his pocket knife.

"Have you been here all night?" Kate said, pouring two mugs of tea. She popped a couple of crumpets into the toaster and grabbed a carton of orange juice from the fridge.

"Of course," Leo said. "Somebody's got to finish this thing." He slotted a tiny piece into place, filling an empty gap in the sky. "Aha, ha." He stood up and stretched. "And now I shall go and muck in my horse."

"Muck *out*," Kate said.

Leo's English was so good that it was hard to remember he came from Holland. Kate knew all of two words in Dutch.

"*Hielen omlaag*," she said. It meant *heels down*.

Leo's eyebrows shot up. "Where'd you learn that?"

"From a book."

"About riding lessons in The Netherlands?"

"No," Kate said. "It's a time travel story about horses and the Civil War. One of the girls is half Dutch."

"Hmmm," Leo said. "Would I enjoy it?"

Kate shrugged. "I dunno. Maybe. It's got a guy in it." She paused. "Lots of guys. Soldiers."

Leo whipped out his iPhone. "What's it called?"

"*Turning on a Dime*," Kate said.

She was edging sideways through the door with her tray and being supercareful not to spill the tea, when Leo announced that he'd downloaded the book. *"Je bent schattig."*

"What does that mean?" Kate said, immediately suspicious.

He grinned. "Look it up."

"How?"

"Google translator."

*　*　*

To Kate's relief, Holly hadn't disappeared. Sitting on the lower bunk, they devoured hot buttered crumpets and shared Holly's orange juice. Kate sipped her tea. "So, what's the plan?"

"We escape."

"Don't be silly," Kate said. "We're not prisoners."

"But Adam and Twiggy are," Holly said. "We've got to do *something*. We can't sit here all day like—"

Bridget stuck her head around the door. "No lessons this morning," she said cheerfully. "Nicole is sick and Will's at a clinic, so we're going on a field trip instead."

"Where to?"

"A tin mine," Bridget said.

Kate flinched. "Does it have pit ponies?"

"Oh, no. The mines have been abandoned for donkey's years. Besides, that was the coal mines, not tin."

"*Donkey's years?*" Kate said.

"Like for*ever*," Bridget explained. "You know . . . yonks and yonks."

"Sounds riveting," Holly said. She waited till Bridget ran off, then rounded on Kate. "I've got an idea."

"What?" Kate said, on full alert. Whenever Holly had an idea, it usually led to trouble, like the time she got the Timber

Ridge team to go trick-or-treating on horseback and it wound up backfiring on Kate.

"While they're at the stupid tin mine," Holly said, plucking her tankini off the floor, "we'll ride to the beach and take the horses swimming."

"We can't."

"Why not?"

"Because I don't have a suit, remember?" Kate said. "It's ripped." They hadn't replaced it, either.

"So borrow one of mine," Holly said.

Kate hesitated. She didn't want to stay cooped up inside anymore than Holly did. Getting up, she peeked out the window. Prince Ferdinand's limo was still in the yard, and who knew how long it would take Jude—and maybe Caroline—to calm him down. All day, probably. Well, at least until lunch time.

Morning feed was now over.

Amid heated arguments over who got to sit up front, the other riders piled into a Beaumont Park van and drove off with Mac. Had Leo gone, too? Kate couldn't be sure. His words rumbled around inside her head. *Ya bend something-or-other?* She'd never be able to figure them out—with or without Google's help.

Holly pulled on a pink t-shirt that said *Boss Mare* on the front, then climbed into her breeches. "You coming?"

"Yeah, sure," Kate said.

Going with her would be a lot less stressful than letting her get in trouble by herself.

* * *

The yard was eerily quiet—most of the horses had been turned out. A couple of grooms were helping a guy unload hay, but they wouldn't know, much less care, that Holly had been grounded.

Feeling like a fugitive, she glanced behind her. No sign of Jude or the prince—just his ugly black limo with poor old Steffan slumped over the wheel fast asleep.

Tiptoeing past, Holly held her breath until she reached Spud's stall. It was pure dumb luck that he and Buccaneer hadn't been turned out as well. They'd never have been able to catch Buccaneer, even with a fistful of Polos.

Spud whickered, just like Magician.

Holly rubbed his ears and fed him a mint. Spud lipped it up, then spat it out.

"Silly boy," she said. "There's nothing else."

After grooming him, Holly checked her phone. No messages, no word from the inspector. Ought she to call him about Prince Ferdinand? But what could he do? He was up in London; the prince was down here and probably blabbing all over Twitter and Facebook by now.

If only she could do something.

But what, exactly? It wasn't as if disobeying Jude and riding to the beach would help Adam and Twiggy.

Or would it?

Maybe if she stopped worrying and just let her mind wander off on its own, an idea or a detail she'd forgotten about would suddenly pop up. She set down her phone and hefted Spud's saddle onto his back. Moments later, she had his bridle on as well.

She led him outside.

Kate was already mounted on Buccaneer; the grooms were still unloading hay. Holly crammed on her helmet, stuck her foot in the stirrup, and landed none too gently in Spud's saddle. She'd take it off the minute they arrived at the beach.

It was lovely and hot—perfect for swimming and nothing like the miserable English weather that Jennifer had warned them about before they'd left Vermont. Holly's green umbrella was gathering dust in the closet.

* * *

The beach was even quieter than the yard had been. No fishermen, no little boys scrambling over rocks and catching crabs in defiance of the *no trespassing* sign. Not even a dog running loose.

Holly shaded her eyes and looked at Smuggler's Island. White-capped waves rippled across the sand bar. Was the tide going out or coming in? Hard to tell. Hooking her right leg over Spud's withers, Holly slid to the ground. Off came his saddle, then her boots, socks, and breeches. She dug her bare toes into a pile of soft, warm sand.

Wonderful.

"Careful," Kate warned. "Spud's clumsy. He might step on you."

"Worrywort," Holly said and dug her toes even deeper. Already she felt better, more at ease. Maybe an idea would hit, maybe—

"Hey, there," said a voice.

Holly whirled around so fast she almost fell over.

Leo? Hadn't he gone with the others?

Still wiggling her toes, Holly forced a smile. He wasn't that bad, really, but why did he have to show up now? A couple of seagulls waddled past. Holly kicked sand at them.

"Not good," Leo said. He rode toward them wearing cut-offs and rubber clogs—no shirt, no saddle.

"Why?" Holly said.

"Because seagulls carry the souls of dead sailors," Leo said. "You don't want to make them angry."

"That's an albatross," Kate said.

Leo shrugged. "Same thing."

Kate looked about ready to argue when something rumbled. Holly glanced toward the horizon. Clouds that hadn't been there five minutes ago were now piling up like dirty gray pillows.

Oh, great. First Leo and now a thunderstorm?

"It's far away," he said. "We have time to swim, so let's go." Wheeling Adonis around like a cowboy, he took off in a shower of sand that annoyed far more gulls than Holly had.

Kate got off Buccaneer and stripped down to the tank suit she'd borrowed from Holly. She parked her saddle on top of her clothes and vaulted back onto Buccaneer. "Sorry about Leo," Kate said.

"Not your fault," Holly replied.

Just then, something else rumbled, louder, closer. More like a roar than thunder. Leo came cantering back. "There's your *pirate* ship," he said, waving toward the island.

Holly gulped as it came into view.

"It's a very fast boat," Leo said. "It will go all the way to Holland."

"How about London?" Holly said. A connection was beginning to form, fuzzy and indistinct. Something she couldn't quite put her finger on.

"Sure," Leo said. "No problem."

With a deep-throated roar, the boat swept in a wide circle across the bay, kicking up a wake that rolled toward them like a miniature tidal wave. Holly caught sight of a man on deck, a flash of black hair.

A beard?

"Oh, my god," she said feeling sick.

"What's wrong?"

Holly could barely get the words out. How could she have been so stupid, so blind? "That man," she said, pointing. "He was driving the limo."

"Prince Ferdinand's?" Kate said.

"No, the one that took Adam and Twiggy. He's the kidnapper." Holly narrowed her eyes. She could see him, right before he rolled up the limo's front window, as dark and ominous as the storm that was now bearing down on them. Why, oh why, hadn't she made the connection before now?

"Which means," Kate said, "that if you're right, Adam and Twiggy are on that boat." She sucked in her breath. "Call the inspector."

"I can't," Holly said, rummaging through her pile of clothes and coming up empty. "I forgot my phone."

"Use mine." Leo dug into his pocket and gave it to her.

Could she remember the inspector's number? As her clumsy fingers hit the wrong keys, she heard Kate telling Leo what was going on. At this point, it didn't matter who knew.

After punching in two more wrong numbers, Holly finally reached Inspector Morgan's voice mail. She left a garbled message because her mouth hadn't yet caught up with her brain. If the inspector tried to call her back, would he use this phone or hers, now lying somewhere in Spud's stall?

"Wait up," Leo said. "There's more."

"What?"

"Tell him it's a Bertram 54, heading south, southeast."

22

THE MOMENT HOLLY FINISHED her call, Leo jumped off Adonis and gave her a leg-up, then climbed back onto his own horse.

"Thanks," Holly said.

For a few seconds, they just sat there, staring at the boat as it became a speck on the horizon that was now piled even higher with thunderous looking clouds. Leo said the Bertram would be traveling at top speed, twenty-eight or thirty knots.

"Where to?" Kate said.

"France, probably," he said. "Normandy or Brittany."

Geography wasn't Kate's strong point, but she knew France was across the English Channel. If only they'd gotten here sooner they could have . . .

Done what, exactly?

Stormed the boat with swords between their teeth like Jack Sparrow in *Pirates of the Caribbean*? They'd watched it

last week in the common room. Twiggy had swooned and declared that Johnny Depp was the best pirate ever.

"I'm going to the island," Holly said. She kicked Spud
hard, and he plunged into the surf. The sand bar was nothing
more than a few white blobs amid churning blue water.

"Don't," Kate yelled. "You'll get stuck."

Even worse, it wouldn't do any good. Twiggy and Adam
were in that boat, not sunbathing on the beach at Smuggler's
Island. No wonder the police hadn't found them. They'd
been looking in all the wrong places.

"The tide's coming in," Leo shouted.

Holly waved him off. "I don't care."

"I'd better go with her." Kate squeezed Buccaneer, and he
shot forward, leaping the waves like a startled rabbit. In
three strides, Leo was beside her. Triumphantly, he held up
his phone as if he'd just won it in a raffle.

"Mustn't get it wet."

The horses were now in deep enough to swim. A wave
rolled toward them, larger than the others, and almost swept
Kate off Buccaneer's slippery back. She clung to his mane. It
rippled across her hands like black seaweed.

Another wave hit and smothered Leo. His arm stuck up
like a submarine's periscope, still attached to his cell phone.
Seconds later, he surfaced, laughing and spitting water.

"You all right?" Kate yelled.

He waved. "*Ja.*"

Ahead of them, Holly and Spud were about to scramble
up the sand bank, now reduced to three isolated humps like
the body of a half-submerged sea monster.

This was totally insane.

From what Kate could see, the island's tiny beach was getting smaller every minute. There'd been a full moon last night. Did that mean a superhigh tide today? Leo would probably know.

Thunder rumbled.

Trying not to panic, Kate glanced back toward the shore. There was no turning around. They were now closer to Smuggler's Island than Pirate's Cove—and about to be stranded in a storm. At least they had Leo's phone.

That is, if he'd managed to keep it dry.

* * *

Raindrops the size of bullets hammered them from all sides. Holly shouted at Spud to keep going. He lowered his head and plowed up the island's beach like a tank.

Ahead was a wall of rocks.

No sign of any caves—just sheer cliffs that even a mountain goat couldn't climb. Shielding her eyes, Holly looked left and right. Was that a path? It was hard to tell. She blinked and looked again.

The wind tore pebbles loose.

Tumbling down, they swirled around Spud's feet like marbles in a pinball machine. But still he didn't freak out. Behind her, Holly could hear Kate and Leo trying to calm their fractious horses.

"Hey, buddy. It's okay."

"Whoa!"

"Follow me," Holly yelled.

She whirled Spud around. The left-hand path looked easier, so up they went, then down, scrambling for traction on hummocks of slippery grass. Despite the wind and rain, Spud didn't put a foot wrong. Jude had said this horse was bulletproof and she wasn't kidding. He was even more bulletproof than good old Marmalade.

Rocks slid from beneath Spud's feet.

Driftwood splintered and shells cracked. But still Spud kept on going—a horse with a mission—just like Sergeant Reckless, an amazing mare Holly had read about who'd braved bullets and bombs in the Korean War to deliver ammunition to the troops.

She patted Spud's neck.

He gave a little sigh and shook his head as if this were no big deal. Holly tried to relax, but as they rounded the next corner all her nerves came to life at once, buzzing about like bees in a bottle.

A sloping beach with two caves.

The upper cave was wide and shallow, barely six feet deep. No sign of any tunnels—just craggy walls with a few tufts of grass and a lone seagull with its head buried beneath one wing, sheltering from the storm.

Holly urged Spud forward.

Down the beach they went, slipping and sliding toward the lower cave. It yawned open like a clown's mouth—dark and mysterious and perfect for hiding stuff you didn't want anyone to find.

Were Adam and Twiggy in there?

A narrow stream of water was already flowing into the

cave, carving sharp edges in the sand as it disappeared from view. How deep would the water get?

Fear prickled Holly's skin. "I'm going in."

"Me, too," Kate yelled.

But her horse had other ideas. Despite Kate's frantic efforts, Buccaneer dug in his toes, whipped around, and snorted like a dragon. So did Adonis. He reared and almost dumped Leo in a tide pool. No way would either horse go anywhere near that scary looking cave.

Spud didn't even hesitate.

He just plunged into the gloom. Beneath his feet, Holly could feel sand giving way to rocks and gravel. This place was totally creepy, like something from the scariest parts of *Moonlight*. When Nathan was on location in New Zealand, he'd sent them videos of the caves they were shooting in. They had tunnels that went on for miles, filled with rare bats. Holly shivered.

"Adam?" she yelled. "Twiggy?"

Nothing, not even an echo.

She pushed further in. The walls narrowed, the roof got lower. It smelled damp and musty, like wet wool, as if a sheep had gotten stranded in here. Something dripped onto Holly's face and slithered down her neck. It got darker and darker.

If only she had a flash—

Her thought wasn't even half formed when a beam of light—intense and focused like a laser—shot into view. For a few seconds, the whole cave lit up. Rocks glistened; prehistoric monsters turned into puppies and kittens.

"It's me," Leo said. He was on foot, waving his phone.

"Where's Adonis?" Holly said.

"Outside, with Kate."

Okay, so now they were two against—what, exactly? Holly had no clue. She yelled again. "Twiggy . . . Adam . . . hello?"

If this were a movie, she'd get an echo, something like *"Lo, lo, lo,"* and her friends would answer with echoes of their own. Cue tumultuous music, crashing symbols, a triumphant choir.

But this wasn't a movie or even a book. It was plain old life, and it wasn't cooperating. The cave darkened; the light on Leo's cell phone flickered.

He grabbed Holly's foot.

"They're not here," he said. "Or they'd have heard us. We should turn back."

"No," Holly said.

She knew, just *knew*, that Twiggy and Adam weren't on that boat. They were in this cave, and Holly was determined to find them. Shaking off Leo's hand, she pushed forward. How Spud kept going without freaking out was a miracle. Maybe he had night vision, like a cat or a raccoon. Or maybe he was dumb as a stump.

Whatever.

At this point, it didn't matter, as long as he kept moving in the right direction. Holly gripped Spud's soaking wet sides even tighter. He grunted.

"Good boy," she whispered.

Out of the eerie silence came a sound.

Whoooooo . . .

An owl? Holly cupped her mouth. "Adam? Twiggy?" No reply—just Leo, crashing up behind her. She reached down. "Give me your phone. I'm going—"

"You will stay here," Leo said, like he was suddenly in charge. "I shall go."

"Forget it," Holly snapped.

"But, you're only a—"

Girl?

Were boys in Holland really this stupid, this far behind the times? "They're *my* friends," Holly said. "You don't even *know* Adam."

"Doesn't matter," Leo said. "I'm sure he'd be happy to see me."

Snorting with exasperation, Holly threw herself off Spud's back and thrust his reins at Leo. It wasn't safe for Spud to wander about loose in a cave. He'd get hurt. "Stay with my horse."

"Why should I?"

"Because you're a . . . a bratface."

"What is this *bratface*?" Leo said, looking puzzled. "Is good, yes?"

"The *best*," Holly said.

She gave him a little push, just enough to throw him off balance, then snatched his phone and scrambled out of reach. Fingers of water licked at her feet. The tide was still coming in. How high would it get? She aimed Leo's light at the walls, dripping wet and hung with fronds of seaweed like Halloween decorations. At any moment, bats would come swooping toward her, or maybe a giant owl. Did they live in caves?

Did spiders?

Jennifer said England had some really big ones.

Trying not to shudder, Holly picked her way across the rocks. Stones and broken shells dug into her bare feet. Something soft brushed against her face. She froze, heart thumping so hard it almost shot out of her mouth.

Must. Not. Scream.

Maybe this wasn't such a hot idea. Maybe she wasn't as brave as she thought. Then a sound—worse than nails on a blackboard amplified a million times—shattered the silence. Head spinning, Holly whirled around, half expecting to see Leo fighting off a giant squid.

Spud whinnied again.

"Phew." Holly's breath came out in such a loud whoosh she almost didn't hear Adam yelling at her to hurry up. It was Adam, wasn't it? She wasn't imagining things—like hearing what she *wanted* to hear?

But Leo heard it, too. "That way," he said.

Boulders covered with barnacles blocked the path. Squeezing between them, Holly gritted her teeth as jagged edges roughed up her skin like a giant cheese grater. Adam called again. She tried to get a fix on his voice, but it seemed to be coming from everywhere at once.

Was he alone? What about Twiggy?

Was there a pirate with them, ready to snatch Holly as

well? She stumbled over a rock and landed on her knees. Leo's phone squirted from her grip like a water balloon. Out went the light.

Oh, great!

Still kneeling, Holly fumbled around in the gloom. Her hand touched something hard and small. The phone? No, a bottle. "Adam, where are you?"

"Over here."

"Where's *here*?" Holly yelled. "Stand up, so—"

"I can't."

"Then throw a stone," she said. "Anything."

"Can't do that, either."

"Okay, so keep talking," Holly said. She would follow his voice, and she'd taken all of two steps toward it when the light from Leo's cell phone sprang into action like a strobe.

"There's something over there," Leo said. "By that big rock." He grabbed Holly's arm and pulled her along, stumbling and tripping. She could barely see her legs, let alone where she was putting her feet.

"What about Spud?" she gasped.

"I let him go."

"But you can't, it's dangerous. He's—"

"He's a horse," Leo said, still holding her arm in a vise grip. "And people are more important."

Holly opened her mouth to argue and shut it again. Leo was right. For better or worse, Spud could fend for himself; Adam and Twiggy couldn't. They were trapped inside this cave, they were—

Here?

Leo's light picked out two shapes huddled beneath a ledge. Ropes bound their wrists and ankles; a filthy gag covered Twiggy's mouth. Her eyes fluttered open, then closed.

"Hurry," Adam groaned.

Water, dark and dirty and relentless, surged forward. For a few seconds, it swirled around their feet like a vortex, then receded and came roaring back—deeper and deeper. Leo squatted beside Adam and whipped out his pocket knife.

"Keep still," he said.

While Leo sawed at the ropes, Holly shone the light on Adam's face. His eyes were red and raw, like he hadn't slept in days or he'd been crying. Probably both. "Thanks," he said in a ragged whisper. "I owe you."

"You bet," she said, feeling sick.

If they got out of this mess in one piece, she would never, ever again bug Adam about leaving Larchwood to ride for Timber Ridge. She would never punch him again, either.

23

WAVES ROLLED UP THE BEACH, breaking closer and closer. Anxiously, Kate scoped out the higher ground. Pretty soon this tiny patch of sand would disappear. The horses had churned it up like a plowed field. Already their hoofprints were half filled with water; the narrow stream flowing into the lower cave had gotten a lot wider.

Leading a reluctant Adonis, Kate urged Buccaneer into ever-tightening circles. How long had Holly and Leo been gone?

Ten minutes? Twenty?

It felt like two hours. Thunder rumbled and lightning cracked, but farther away. The storm had eased up, just a little—not that the horses noticed. Nostrils flaring, Adonis showed the whites of his eyes. Buccaneer snorted and tossed his head.

"Easy boy," Kate said.

Rain pummeled her shoulders; the wind whipped her hair into a frenzy. She could barely feel her fingers, permanently frozen around both sets of slippery reins. Her feet were totally numb.

They needed shelter.

But Buccaneer refused to go anywhere near the shallow cave. He whirled around like a windup toy gone mad. Adonis crashed into him. The lone seagull, still on its rocky perch, gave them all a beady-eyed stare.

Idiots, it said.

Kate lowered her head against the wind. As long as Buccaneer didn't toss her off, she would keep going, around and around, and watching the cave until—

Spud trotted out.

Calm as a police horse, he surveyed the beach, then reached up and cropped a clump of grass from the cliff. The seagull flew off, squawking. Moments later, Leo emerged from the cave with Twiggy in his arms.

It all happened in slow motion.

Twiggy's blond hair was a tangled mess; her white gown in shreds. Eyes closed, it looked as if she'd passed out, or—

"Is she—?" Kate faltered.

Leo said, "She is okay."

"What about Adam?"

"Holly's got him."

Kate half expected Holly to be carrying Adam the way Leo carried Twiggy, but Adam limped from the cave, leaning hard on Holly. His shirt was torn; his tuxedo looked as if giant moths had attacked it.

He gave Kate a feeble grin as Holly steered him toward Twiggy, now sitting in the shallow cave with Leo fussing over her like a mother hen.

Twiggy worked her jaw back and forth. "Yuck, that gag was disgusting."

"Why did they gag you and not Adam?" Holly said.

Adam rubbed his wrists. "Because she gave them a hard time."

"And you didn't?"

Leo pulled out his cell phone. "What's the emergency number?"

"Nine, nine, nine," Holly said.

A gust of wind sent shells and dry seaweed tumbling across what was left of the beach. Was the tide still coming in? As Buccaneer spooked at harmless rocks, Kate crossed her stiffened fingers. Would Leo even get cell service in a storm like this?

* * *

He tried for twenty minutes, but nothing worked—not even climbing to the island's highest point in case there was a signal up there.

"We must swim back," he said.

The tide had already turned, so that was in their favor. But there were now five of them and only three horses. How would they feel about carrying two riders at once? Kate wasn't sure if Buccaneer would tolerate it. She knew Adonis wouldn't.

"We'll have to double up," Holly said.

Leo helped Twiggy to her feet. "I'll take the princess."

"My knight in shining armor," she muttered.

Adam protested. "Hey, I thought that was *me*."

He'd already told them the kidnappers were total jerks. "Worse than the Three Stooges," he'd said as they huddled in the alcove and waited for Leo find a cell signal. Then Twiggy said it was like being stuck in an Enid Blyton adventure.

"What's that?" Holly said.

"The British version of *Nancy Drew Meets The Hardy Boys*," Kate said.

Her mother had a collection of old Enid Blyton books she'd brought with her from England, and Kate loved them—especially the ones about a girl who took her horse to boarding school. His name was Thunder, which seemed kind of appropriate right now.

After they straggled back to the island's main beach, Holly insisted that Leo ride Spud. "He's the safest horse," she said. "The others will freak out."

"What about you and Adam?" Leo said, as he hoisted Twiggy on board and vaulted up behind her.

"He can ride Adonis, and I'll swim."

"Swim?" Leo said. "But—"

Kate was about to tell him that Holly could outswim all of them, including the horses, when she heard the whup-whup-whup of a helicopter. She looked up, but the cloud cover was too dense to see anything. Was that the police?

Had the inspector gotten Holly's message?

"It's got to be them," Holly said. "I mean, who else would be flying in weather like this?"

Leo agreed, then said the Bertram couldn't have gone more than thirty miles, maybe less. It would be easy for a chopper to catch.

"How?" Kate said.

She had visions of a giant net flung out by the helicopter and scooping up the pirates like butterflies. No, not butterflies. More like sharks or piranha fish. But Leo explained they'd hover over the boat and order it into the nearest port. If it refused, they'd drop agents on board.

"With guns?" Kate said. It all sounded so improbable, like a really bad spy movie or a nightmare she'd wake up from at any minute.

Leo grinned. "Bang, bang."

Pinning him with a look, Holly climbed onto a rock and plunged into the waves like a dolphin. Parts of the sand bar were starting to show. Adam let out a faint whoop and kicked Adonis. Into the water they went. Then came Leo with his arms wrapped so tightly around Twiggy she'd probably be adding sore ribs to her other woes.

Kate and Buccaneer went last.

The cold took her breath away. Teeth chattering, Kate twisted her numb fingers into Buccaneer's mane. As long as they avoided the current, they'd be okay. She fixed her eyes on the beach. That's where her clothes were, and she couldn't wait to get into them . . . and sit by a roaring fire in the common room.

Yes, it was the middle of July. But right now it felt like December, and to make matters worse, a fog was rolling in.

* * *

The rogue wave hit when they were half way to Pirate's Cove. It swamped everyone, including Leo whose arms were still wrapped around Twiggy. But seconds later when they surfaced, Spud had disappeared. No sign of him. Not even an ear.

Leo yelled at Kate. "I'm going in."

He held Twiggy with one arm in life-saving mode and swam toward the beach. Her white dressed billowed in and out like a jellyfish. Feeling helpless, Kate watched them go. Leo couldn't abandon Twiggy to search for Spud. She was too weak to manage on her own.

"Spud," Kate screamed.

It was like the ocean had swallowed him whole. She yelled again, but the wind whipped her words away. Nobody but her and Leo, and maybe Twiggy, knew what happened. Adam and Holly were too far ahead to hear their cries over the pounding waves. They wouldn't know Spud was missing until they saw Leo without him.

But what could they do?

Kate searched for a sign—anything that would tell her Spud was okay. But the waves were too high. Even if Spud's head was well above the surface, she wouldn't be able to see it. She had to find him.

She absolutely *had* to.

Frantically, she hauled on the reins, but Buccaneer wouldn't turn. Or maybe he couldn't. Had they caught the edge of the current? Kate felt them being swept along, parallel to the shore, and unable to fight it. Feeling even more helpless, Kate clung to Buccaneer's neck and hoped the current would let them go before it smashed them onto the rocks.

* * *

If Holly were grading her own performance, she'd give herself a C-minus for that swim. Maybe a D. Exhausted, she collapsed onto the hard-packed sand and curled into a ball, breathing hard. She hadn't been this wiped out since doing all those killer exercises after she'd begun walking again last year.

Even her toenails hurt.

With a groan, Holly forced herself to sit up. The rain slanted sideways, sandblasting her face and scouring her eyeballs. She rubbed them, but she still couldn't see more than ten feet. Waves, rain, and fog had melded into a ghostly gray mass. Then, out of the gloom, Adam wobbled into view like a mirage in the desert—all shimmery and out-of-focus.

Holly rubbed her eyes again. "You okay?"

"I think so."

Adam slithered off Adonis like a limp puppet and landed beside her. Holly heaved a sigh of relief. The others couldn't be far behind. But her relief turned to fear when Leo staggered out of the water carrying Twiggy.

Holly scrambled to her feet. "Where's Spud?"

"That big wave." Leo's breath came in short gasps. "We went under for a bit and then Spud, well, he—"

"What?"

Gently, Leo set Twiggy down. She slumped against Adam. "He disappeared."

"Don't be crazy," Holly snapped. "Horses just don't disappear." She caught her breath. "Where's Kate?"

"Still on Buccaneer, last I saw."

"Where?"

"Behind me," Leo said. "They'll be here in a minute."

"We need help," Holly said, squinting toward where she figured the horizon would be if she could actually see it. "Where's your phone?"

"Right here," Leo said, shaking it so hard that water flew out. "But it's useless."

"And so are you."

The moment her words were out, Holly wanted to bite them back. Leo wasn't useless. He'd saved Twiggy—saved them all, really—with his phone and that pocket knife. "I'm sorry," she blurted. "But—"

A shallow wave rolled toward them. "Come on," Leo said. "We'd better get higher up the beach. Then we'll figure out what to do."

"I already know," Holly said, as she helped Leo with Adam and Twiggy. "You're going to ride Adonis back to the yard for help, and I'm going to look for Kate—and Spud."

"You can't," Leo said.

"Try and stop me." Holly piled towels and clothes on top of Adam and Twiggy, now shivering uncontrollably. "And tell Mac to bring the trailer."

Then, before Leo had a chance to argue, Holly took off

down the beach. Jennifer had said the current always ran from left to right, so if Kate and the two horses had been caught in it, they'd be heading straight for the rocks.

24

BUCCANEER HEARD IT FIRST. Ears pricked, he turned his head toward the beach and gave a shrill whinny. Was it Spud? Kate pulled her right rein as hard as she could. She hated being rough with Buccaneer, but she'd make it up to him later with lots of Polos, once they—

"Kate? Where are you?"

Holly's disembodied voice floated through the gloom. Vaguely, Kate remembered learning that sound traveled farther on water than on land, so while it felt like Holly was close by, she could be hundreds of yards away.

"Here," Kate yelled back.

That's what everyone said, and it was totally stupid. How would Holly know where *here* was? If only she could see her, give her a landmark like "third rock on the left" or "in front of that big wave." But that was even sillier. Fear and cold had numbed her brain along with her fingers.

She yelled again.

Briefly, the fog thinned, and there was Holly swimming toward her. For a second or two she disappeared behind a wave, then she bobbed up again like a rubber duck. Kate had never been so relieved to see anyone in her life.

Holly trod water, keeping well away from Buccaneer's thrashing legs. "Did you find Spud?"

"No," Kate said. "I tried, but—"

"It's all my fault," Holly wailed. "We've *got* to find him."

"We can't," Kate said, thinking fast. Somehow, she had to stop Holly from swimming out to sea, even if it meant lying. "The lifeboats will rescue him."

"How?"

Kate had no idea. "A big winch, with straps for his belly—and a skin diver." Even to her ears, it sounded ridiculous. But it must've worked because a couple of seconds later Holly turned and began swimming back to shore.

Buccaneer followed.

The wind had died down, and the waves weren't quite as scary as before. Even the current had backed off or gone somewhere else. Slowly, the fog lifted and the beach came into focus. Kate could see Adam and Twiggy, wrapped in towels and huddled together like a couple of castaways.

Holly said that Leo had gone for help.

It arrived as Kate rode Buccaneer out of the water. He shook himself so violently that she tumbled off and landed like a pancake in the sand.

Jude got there first.

Sloshing through tide pools in green wellies, she helped Kate to her feet. "You all right?" she said, wrapping her in a blanket. It was itchy and smelled comfortingly of horse.

Kate couldn't stop shivering. "I think so, but—"

"Leo told me about Spud."

"Will he—?"

"Horses are strong," Jude said, rubbing Kate's hands with her much larger ones. "And they're pretty good swimmers. He's probably over at Half Moon Beach, chatting up the tourists."

A big lie, same as the whopper she'd told Holly.

After that, everything blurred like a watercolor left out in the rain. Kate couldn't keep track any more. She heard voices, saw people milling about. Mac examined Buccaneer's legs, then threw a blanket over his back and loaded him onto the trailer. An ambulance arrived, sirens wailing louder than fire alarms. Two medics leaped out and strapped Adam and Twiggy onto stretchers.

"No, I'm okay," Adam protested. "Really."

"Don't argue, mate," one of the medics said and hefted Adam, still protesting, into the ambulance beside Twiggy.

Did her father know about this?

Was Prince Ferdinand still at Beaumont Park, throwing his weight around? There were so many questions Kate wanted to ask, but she couldn't quite summon up the energy. All she wanted was sleep—and to be warm again.

* * *

The grooms organized a search party for Spud. Holly begged to go with them, but Jude wouldn't let her.

"You're wiped out," she said, sounding stern. "You'd be more of a hindrance than a help. Take a hot shower and get some rest."

Instead, Holly let herself into Spud's empty stall, retrieved her cell phone, then sat down and cried. Inspector Morgan had left two messages. The first one said that his crew was already in the air.

The second, three hours later, said:

We caught them. Ring me back.

Holly punched in the inspector's number. He answered on the first ring and said that the kidnappers had confessed and told his policemen where to find Adam and Twiggy. The chopper was about to land on Smuggler's Island.

"Too late," Holly said. "We found them."

It felt kind of weird to be telling Inspector Morgan what to do instead of listening to him issue instructions. When she got through giving him a blow-by-blow account of rescuing Adam and Twiggy, there was a brief silence.

"You're an amazing young woman," he finally said. "Courageous, too."

Holly didn't feel amazing, much less courageous. She was a total failure for losing Spud. It was the one thing she could not bring herself to tell the inspector about. If she hadn't dragged Twiggy off to London, Spud would be out in the field or in his stall waiting for her to bring him a carrot. Better yet, they'd be tacking up for a lesson with Will or Nicole.

The awfulness of it all slammed into Holly the moment she hung up. Feeling sick, she replayed the inspector's last words, over and over, in her mind.

"If you hadn't found them," he'd said, "Adam and Twiggy would've drowned."

That was the kidnappers' plan.

Once they discovered they had the wrong kids, they had to get rid of them—and what better way than tied up in a cave that flooded at high tide? The locals never went there, and the few tourists who did walked across the sand bar and then scurried back to Pirate's Cove before the water got too deep. According to what Holly had heard, nobody ever went around the other side of the island—not on foot anyway.

Exhaustion overwhelmed her. She didn't dare sleep for fear of missing news about Spud, but maybe if she just closed her eyes for a few minutes, it would help.

* * *

Kate tried to rest. She tossed and turned, but sleep wouldn't come. So she got up and tried, yet again, to compose a text message to her father and Liz about the kidnapping.

It would send them into orbit.

They'd probably order the girls to come home right away. Best to wait until she and Holly had access to a computer and could write a proper e-mail.

Kate pocketed her phone, then slouched downstairs to look for Holly and see if there was any news about Spud. The grooms had already come back empty-handed, but Jennifer and Bridget were still out scouring the neighborhood. Kate found Jude in the tack room, gathering up saddle pads and blankets for the laundry.

"Have you seen Holly?" Kate said.

"I sent her upstairs for a shower."

"When?"

"Two hours ago," Jude said. "Go ask Leo and the others. They might know where she is."

Margot and Harriet were in the common room playing video games, and Zoe was painting her nails. They shrugged and said they hadn't seen Holly since the night before. Kate finally tracked Leo down in Adonis's stall, but he had no clue where Holly had gone.

"Did you ever figure it out?" he said.

"What?"

"*Je bent schattig.*"

"Oh, that." Kate had forgotten all about it. "So, what does it mean?"

Rubbing Adonis between the eyes, Leo said, "You are cute."

"Yes, he is," Kate said. "But—"

Leo grinned at her.

"Oh," Kate said as the penny dropped.

So, of course, she blushed . . . the way she always did. Maybe that's what Leo wanted, to embarrass her. His laughter followed her down the yard as she bolted into Buccaneer's stall. She didn't know what to think about Leo, she really didn't. Right now it was probably best not to think about him at all.

The grooms got busy with evening feed, but nobody was

chatting or whistling. The place felt like a morgue. Even the horses were quieter than usual, almost as if they sensed one of their buddies was missing. Kate fed Buccaneer the Polos she'd promised and was about to pitch in and help with chores when horses clattered into the yard. Not daring to hope, Kate looked up.

"Oh, my god," she cried. "Where did you find him?"

"Half Moon Beach," Jennifer said. She jumped off Renegade and handed Spud's lead rope to Kate.

"But the grooms said he wasn't there."

"Some kids had hidden him behind an enormous camper," Bridget said. "They didn't want to give him up, either."

Evening feed got put on hold as everyone gathered around the returning hero. Mac removed the remnants of Spud's bridle and examined him from ears to tail. "Just a few scratches," he said. "Put some antiseptic ointment on them, and feed him some dinner. He's earned it."

Overjoyed, Kate led the irrepressible Spud into his stall, wishing that Holly were here. This should've been her doing this, but—

Spud lowered his head.

He whickered and nuzzled someone curled up in a pile of shavings.

* * *

Something soft tickled Holly's cheek. She pushed it away, then leaned into Spud's flying mane as he jumped the waves.

Dolphins swam on both sides, leaping about like exuberant puppies. On the horizon, a double rainbow beckoned. Yes, she would ride Spud to that.

They'd find a pot of gold, and—

Whatever it was that had been tickling her did it again. She opened her eyes and blinked.

Spud?

Was it him, like for real?

Feeling dizzy, Holly sat up. She heard Kate laughing and babbling that Jennifer and Bridget had found Spud at Half Moon Beach where some kids had hidden him behind a camper, and that Mac had said he's fine, really fine. Just a few scratches, that's all.

Kate flopped down beside her. "Are you okay?"

"I am now." Holly couldn't stop grinning.

With a deep, whuffling sigh, Spud rested his head in her lap. Holly stroked his velvety nose and cried all over again.

* * *

After supper, Jude dropped Holly and Kate at the hospital. Adam was happily reunited with his worried parents and he'd be flying back home with them in the morning. Holly planted a kiss on his cheek and promised never to punch him again—ever.

"Yeah, right," Adam said with a lopsided grin. "Like, I believe you?"

So, of course, she punched him.

His mother hugged Holly and thanked her for rescuing

him. Kate doubted Twiggy's father would do the same. His limo had been parked at the curb when they arrived which meant he was in Twiggy's room, probably bawling her out for sneaking off with Holly.

Poor Twiggy. She couldn't catch a break where her father was concerned. No matter what she did, it was wrong. Kate expected her to be in tears when they got there, but to her surprise Twiggy looked pretty good for someone who'd just been kidnapped, tied up and dumped in a cave, and rescued on horseback in the middle of a thunderstorm.

On her bedside table sat a bouquet of yellow roses. Kate sniffed—they smelled a whole lot better than regular hospital smells—and glanced at the gift card.

To Belle, from the Beast.

But it didn't bother Kate a bit. Nathan's apology—delivered by Holly—had wrapped it all up. They could now be friends, and Kate felt good about that. She also felt good that Twiggy had met Nathan and had fun, even if it had turned into the scariest three days of her life. She had a feeling Twiggy would agree.

Her father cleared his throat.

Kate tensed up, waiting for a stream of insults, but none came. Instead, the prince took Holly's hand and thanked her for saving his daughter.

"How can I make it up to you?" he said.

Watching Holly's mouth fall open, Kate tried to reconcile this version of Prince Ferdinand with the bully she'd met yesterday morning. Gone was the bluster, the bluff, and the disdainful sneer, and he wasn't nearly as big as she remembered.

Finally, Holly found her tongue. "You can give Twiggy back her old horse."

"Diamond?" Twiggy squealed.

Was that her horse's name? Kate had never asked. She didn't think Holly had either. Neither of them had talked to Twiggy about it because they figured it was off limits, a forbidden subject.

"But what about Gemini?" the prince said.

"Offer him to Beaumont Park," Holly shot back. "I'm sure Caroline would buy him."

The prince turned to his daughter. "Well?"

"Oh, yes," she said. "Please."

Even though it was after business hours, Prince Ferdinand whipped out his phone and within minutes the deal was done. "Diamond will be sent to Mr. King on Saturday," he said.

Kate recoiled in horror. "But you can't do that. Vincent King's a *criminal*. He's a terrible trainer. Send Diamond to Will Hunter at Beaumont Park, and let Twiggy have lessons there."

"Well," the prince said looking from Kate to Holly. "You girls have an answer for everything."

"So, just do it," Twiggy said, then added, "Daddy."

The prince sucked in his breath, as if he'd never been called that before—at least, not like this. With an astonished look at Twiggy, he pulled her into an awkward hug. He had tears in his eyes. So did Twiggy.

Kate wanted to hug them both.

She knew what it felt like. Her own father had taken a long time to learn how to be a parent. He was still learning, and he didn't always get it right. But Kate loved him anyway, even if he was totally clueless about Liz.

As if on cue, Holly's cell phone buzzed—a text from her mother. "They want us to come home."

"Why?" Kate said.

Had they found out about the kidnapping? Maybe Adam's parents told them. His mom was friends with Liz.

Holly held up her phone. "This."

At first, it didn't register—a photo of someone's hand with short fingernails and a square-cut diamond surrounded by tiny sapphires. Kate looked closer. She *knew* that ring. It had belonged to her mother who'd left strict instructions in her will that Kate's father should give it to the woman he would one day marry.

"You mean—?"

"It's Mom," Holly said, breaking into the biggest smile Kate had ever seen. "She's going to marry your dad."

About the Author

MAGGIE DANA'S FIRST RIDING LESSON, at the age of five, was less than wonderful. She hated it so much, she didn't try again for another three years. But all it took was the right horse and the right instructor and she was hooked.

After that, Maggie begged for her own pony and was lucky enough to get one. Smoky was a black New Forest pony who loved to eat vanilla pudding and drink tea, and he became her constant companion. Maggie even rode him to school one day and tethered him to the bicycle rack . . . but not for long because all the other kids wanted pony rides, much to their teachers' dismay.

Maggie and Smoky competed in Pony Club trials and won several ribbons. But mostly, they had fun—trail riding and hanging out with other horse-crazy girls. At horse camp, Maggie and her teammates spent one night sleeping in the barn, except they didn't get much sleep because the horses snored. The next morning, everyone was tired and cranky, especially when told to jump without stirrups.

Born and raised in England, Maggie now makes her home on the Connecticut shoreline. When not mucking stalls or grooming shaggy ponies, Maggie enjoys spending time with her family and writing the next book in her TIMBER RIDGE RIDERS series.

16694179R00142

Made in the USA
Middletown, DE
19 December 2014